Shane's Hideaway

by

Sheridon Smythe

Shane's Hideaway

Cover Art by *Kim Mendoza*

The Wild Rose Press
PO Box 706
Adams Basin, NY 14410-0706
Visit us at www.thewildrosepress.com

Publishing History
First Crimson Rose Edition, 2007
Print ISBN 1-60154-134-1

Published in the United States of America

Dedication

I would like to dedicate this book to my wonderful writer friend, Beth Szabo, who pulled my head out of the sand and turned me on to e-publishing. I can't wait to hold your first published book in my hands (or see it on my computer screen) and say 'I told you so'!

What people are saying about Sheridon Smythe...

Mr. Complete
"Sprinkled liberally with laugh-out-loud scenes, and not one but several yummy hunks, this fast-paced story will keep you engrossed to the last page."—Romantic Times

"Humorous and hunk-heaven, Sheridon Smythe spins a delightful tale."—Midwest Book Review

"MR. COMPLETE is absolutely, positively HOT. Sheridon Smythe has written another sexy, hilarious romance that will keep you laughing out loud and have the windows fogging up. From the sexy characters to a definitely unique plot, this book is a perfect 10 all the way around."—Romance Reviews Today

"This will become many a fan's favourite ... it will make you a fan of her hot, steamy, and completely wonderful romances!"—A Romance Review

Hot Number
"HOT NUMBER is a fast-moving story with loads of sexual pressure and plenty of hot scenes ... a light and humorous tale."—RT BOOKclub

"... An engaging romance ... For a thoroughly entertaining read, I recommend HOT NUMBER."—Romance Reviews Today

"HOT NUMBER moves at a fast pace, and gives us lots of chuckles ... a great read that any fan of contemporary romance won't want to miss."—A Romance Review

Chapter One

"I can't deny it any longer." Leandra Dehart peered through the windshield at the swirling white curtain of snow nearly obscuring the unfamiliar landscape. As the implications sank in, the bottom dropped out of her stomach. "We're lost in a blizzard. In the Smokey Mountains. On a side road going to nowhere." She cast a quick, apologetic glance in the rearview mirror at her mute passenger.

Solemn brown eyes stared back at her. Right now they were free of accusation, but Leandra didn't know how long that would last. Eventually, hunger would bring out the beast.

Leandra felt the need to explain herself. "I wanted to surprise them by arriving early. You understand, don't you? And you know we wouldn't be lost right now if I hadn't left my purse in that restroom back on the interstate. I had to go back to see if someone nice—someone decent and honest— had found it and turned it in." The knot of panic in her throat grew. "If only I had checked the weather before we left Galveston. If only I weren't so impulsive and reckless and—" She hit the steering wheel with her frozen fingers.

It hurt, but she deserved it.

If Alec found out..."We...we just need to find a place to turn around," Leandra said, deliberately pushing Alec from her mind. "Once we get back onto the interstate, we'll be fine."

But things didn't look fine. It took every ounce of her energy and skill to keep the PT Cruiser between the lines of trees bordering the narrow road. If they *did* come across a drive or a side road, she doubted she'd see it until it was too late.

Her brother would never forgive her. Never. Nor would he trust her with Molly again, and Leandra didn't blame him. She wasn't a trustworthy person.

Just ask Alec. He'd be all too happy to list her flaws.

Leandra's lips tightened. Alec was a criminal lawyer, defending the slime of society. He could use his words to beat a person to death—or make them *wish* they were dead.

It was hard not to admire him in action, yet impossible to forget the nature of his profession. Sometimes it frightened her to think she might someday work opposite Alec in a courtroom.

She glanced at the gold wedding band on her finger, standing out in stark relief against her whitened skin where she gripped the wheel. How would her brother react to the news? He would be surprised, she mused. And hurt because she'd kept it from him.

But he'd get over it. He'd have to, because it was done.

If she ever saw her brother again.

This had to be the biggest blunder of her life. Bigger, even, than marrying an obsessed, narcissistic asshole like Alec.

She was lost in a blizzard in the Smokey Mountains of North Carolina, hundreds of miles from home. Incredible, even with her impressive track record.

But her precious cargo made this screw up the mother of all screw ups.

She rubbed her cold nose and sniffed, as tears of self-pity welled in her eyes. "Okay," she admitted out loud. "I shouldn't have turned around. I should have forgotten about the four hundred in cash, my driver's license and my credit cards. All of that stuff can be replaced." She flicked a tearful glance in the rearview mirror. Her heart kicked hard against her breastbone when she met the trusting gaze of her passenger. "But you, on the other hand, can not be replaced. You are very special, which is why I was trying to get you home early. They sounded so depressed and lost without you over the phone, and I *know* you've missed them."

Her passenger offered her an innocent, sleepy smile.

Leandra swallowed a sob. Disgusted with herself, she tightened her grip on the wheel as the PT Cruiser began to climb a steep hill, the tires scrambling for traction. She was afraid to slow down, afraid the wheels might become bogged. Already, they hummed eerily with the effort of plowing through the snow.

The animal appeared out of nowhere. Leandra's eyes widened. She hunched over the wheel, trying to identify the animal through the thick, swirling snow. A deer? A dog? As the PT Cruiser drew closer, she realized it *was* a dog. A big, red dog the *size* of a deer.

A dog, right in the middle of the road.

And it wasn't moving out of her way.

Inhaling sharply, Leandra tapped on the brakes as hard as she dared, silently urging the dog to come to his senses and move. The back wheels began a slow slide to the right, giving her heart a painful jolt. Finally, the wheels caught traction and the PT Cruiser jerked straight again.

The dog remained standing in her path, staring into the headlights as if mesmerized. Leandra had read about wild animals freezing at headlights, but a dog? She honked her horn frantically, but the animal didn't budge.

She was going to hit him, she realized in horror. Trembling, Leandra edged the wheel to the left, praying she could ease the PT Cruiser to the side of the road, praying there wasn't a ditch hidden by the snow.

There was no ditch, but she saw too late that there *was* a tree, its thick trunk nearly hidden by a snow drift. Helplessly, she braced herself, her mind screaming in terror as the PT Cruiser's headlights illuminated the new obstacle in their path.

A cry surfaced, bubbled in her throat. She gave no thought to her own safety. *Oh, dear God! Molly!*

****

Shane Knox awoke with a start, sweat glazing his fading summer tan. His entire body trembled, and his chest heaved as if he'd been running for miles without pause. Whatever had awakened him, he was grateful.

He'd been dreaming about Sandra Dillon again, images so vivid it was hard to dispel them even now. It had been over a year since her death, but the nightmares continued to torment him with regularity. Nothing less than he deserved after failing to protect her, he mused with a bitter grimace.

Sitting as still in the worn, comfortable recliner as his trembling body would allow, he listened to the whistling wind, the crackling fire, the faint hum of the generator out back. He discarded each sound, knowing instinctively that none of them had disturbed his sleep.

And then it came again—the deep, urgent barking of a dog.

Buck had found something.

Shane pushed himself from the chair and quickly fastened the top button of his jeans. He shrugged into a flannel shirt and grabbed his deerskin coat from the rack by the door, his hand hovering near the leather shoulder strap housing his gun. Ten years as a police officer made it hard for him to go anywhere without it. But finally, he dropped his hand away and headed out into the dark night and the cold, furious snow.

Hopefully, Buck had caught a rabbit. It would make a welcome change from his never-ending supply of chicken noodle soup.

The three-room, rustic log cabin stood alone at the top of a hill, sheltered by a thick forest of blue firs. Shane's boots sank into the deep snow as he came to the edge of the yard and looked down. Here the road dropped away sharply, making it difficult for vehicles to maneuver in bad weather.

This frustrated most, but suited Shane; he liked his solitude. The captain had thought to punish him by ordering a temporary suspension, when in fact, Shane agreed he needed this time alone. Things *had* gotten out of hand, but when he'd seen that poor woman...he'd nearly lost it.

She had reminded him of Sandra. And the guy— the guy had reminded him of that low-life Bobby Dillon.

Another furious spate of barking caught Shane's attention. He smiled, peering through the dense snow. Buck was all the company a loner like himself needed—

His smile dropped away when he caught sight of the weak glow of headlights piercing the darkness. Who? Had someone defied the weather and attempted to drive up the mountain? Shane frowned at the possibility, pulling his coat collar around his ears and thrusting his bare hands into the warm pockets.

He began to descend his little mountain with the confident ease born from years of experience, not once stumbling, not once hesitating. The bitter cold urged Shane on, knowing whoever was in the car would soon be feeling the same cold.

After several hundred yards, the road began to flatten out and Shane picked up speed. His breath made short bursts of steam in the air, and the snow began to stick to his eyelashes and his hair, piling around the collar of his coat.

He shook it off, keeping his eyes on the yellow glow ahead. Finally, he could make out Buck's brawny shape, then the blunt outline of a vehicle. Buck danced and barked excitedly, seeming oblivious to the fierce blizzard.

As Shane approached the PT Cruiser, he saw the engine still idled. Steam rose from the busted radiator, so apparently the accident had not happened long ago. Checking the passenger door, he found it locked. He trudged through the deep snow to the other side and tried the driver's door. To his immense relief, the door handle gave way.

Straining against the howling wind, Shane pushed the door wide, automatically catching the limp body of a woman as she tumbled out.

He quickly checked her pulse, hoping his fingers weren't too numb to feel the beat. It was there— faint, but steady. With his heart hammering inside his chest, Shane gathered her more fully into his arms and prepared to carry her up the mountain. Thank God, she wasn't that heavy. Not yet, anyway. He considered himself in decent shape, but that was a damned steep hill....

"Come on Buck!" he shouted over the vicious wind.

But Buck didn't obey. Instead, he continued to bark sharply, and then, to Shane's amazement, the big dog jumped through the open doorway of the PT Cruiser onto the front seat.

Shane paused with his burden and stared impatiently at the dog. Obviously, Buck had something else on his mind. Probably a half-eaten hamburger or a sandwich.

He tried again. "Get down, Buck! Come on!"

Buck whined and barked, pointing his snout in

the direction of the back seat.

Stifling an urge to leave him, Shane retraced his steps and looked inside the PT Cruiser to pacify the dog. He didn't expect to find anyone because the woman had been alone in the front seat. Surely if someone was with her, they wouldn't be in the back—

His gaze widened on the baby seat. Beneath the dull glow of the dome light, a pair of dark, curious eyes studied Buck from the furry folds of a hooded snowsuit. After a moment, the little round face turned in his direction and gave him the same, intense regard.

Shane felt his stomach bottom out. A child—a baby! How was he—what was he—he couldn't carry them both—

His jumbled thoughts ground to a halt. He couldn't carry both of them, but he couldn't leave *either* of them. It was too cold, and if he left Buck with the baby while he carried the unconscious woman to the cabin, something might happen to him and the baby would be alone. In this weather, a small child would freeze in no time.

And if he took the baby first, who would look after it at the cabin while he came back for the woman? Shane glanced at the burden in his arms, wishing the snow would ease long enough for him to check her injuries.

What to do? *Hell.* He didn't need this.

He backed out of the PT Cruiser and peered at the collision site. Steam continued to hiss from the radiator, but the engine idled smoothly. It would heat up soon, though, Shane knew. Would the Cruiser make it up the incline?

The baby cooed at Buck. The big dog barked in response, which in turn made the baby laugh. Shane wondered if he dreamed again, for the entire situation seemed too bizarre to be real. A blizzard, an unconscious woman...and a baby's pure, spontaneous laughter? He shook his head, realizing his arms had grown numb from the woman's weight.

Deciding he didn't have much choice, Shane ordered Buck into the back with the baby while he settled his burden into the passenger seat. Buck cheerfully obliged and immediately began to lick the baby's face. The child squealed with unrestrained laughter, blessedly unaware of the critical situation. As Shane listened to the wondrous sound, his lips twitched in response.

How could he think of smiling? They were in the middle of a freak snow storm, a woman was injured—possibly seriously—and he wasn't certain if the PT Cruiser would make it another foot, much less all the way to the cabin.

But the PT Cruiser didn't let him down, despite the death-rattling sound coming from the engine by the time he coaxed it into the garage alongside his own four-wheel drive truck.

He cut the engine and let out a shaky sigh. Those last few yards had been hairy, with the wheels spinning uselessly and the PT Cruiser sliding back down the hill a few heart-stopping feet before gaining traction....

With the engine off, the interior of the PT Cruiser began to cool rapidly. Shane carried the woman inside and laid her on the couch in front of the fire before returning for the baby. Buck seemed to know his duty, for he stayed put until Shane gathered the baby in his arms and backed out of the PT Cruiser. The dog then bounded after them, tail wagging as he raced to the door.

The snow came down relentlessly. Shane pulled his coat over the child and hurried inside, shutting the door on the fierce winter storm that hadn't been in the forecast.

With the immediate crisis over, Shane took a

moment to regain his bearings, holding the baby against his heart. Was it only moments ago that he was thinking how much he enjoyed the solitude storms signified? And now...now there was a woman on his couch and a baby inside his coat.

Buck ran out of patience. He barked, wagged his tail vigorously, then jumped on Shane. Shane staggered back against the door, trying to scowl at the over-zealous dog.

"Get down, you mutt! You'll scare the baby."

A muffled giggle from inside the coat made him a liar.

Buck heard it, too. He scratched at Shane's coat, whining and barking until Shane had no choice but to unwrap the baby for Buck's inspection. As he presented the baby—dressed in a *pink* snow suit, Shane noted—Buck's tongue lagged toward the floor. Shane could have sworn the dog smiled.

"Gently, Buck. It's a baby, not a puppy. A girl, I think." He felt awkward—he didn't have much experience with little ones.

Shane set the baby on the area rug behind the sofa, away from the fireplace. Maybe she wouldn't figure out how to bypass the furniture. Still, he and Buck would keep a sharp eye on her. He wondered how old she was...seven months? A year?

Leaving the baby with Buck, he turned on a second lamp and knelt beside the woman. She lay exactly where he'd placed her. Shane frowned, smoothing the short, dark brown hair away from a face far too pale for his comfort. His fingers stilled as he uncovered a nasty bump on the right side of her forehead. She must have hit the steering wheel, he thought, wondering why the air bag hadn't deployed. He probed the bump, deciding it was a good thing the skin wasn't broken. His emergency medical experience didn't include stitching wounds.

On the other side of the sofa, Buck raced around

the sitting baby, skidded to a halt, and barked. Each time he barked, the baby giggled, and apparently Buck enjoyed the game, for he repeated it again and again.

Bemused, Shane shook his head, then got down to the business of making the woman comfortable. He decided it would be too dangerous trying to make it to the hospital, which was in Asheville, some forty miles away. Without the baby, he might have chanced it, and if she didn't awaken soon, he'd *have* to chance it.

But not unless it was absolutely necessary—for all their sakes. Attempting to go out in this blizzard would be sheer suicide.

With that decision made, Shane gently removed the woman's coat, a thin, supple leather garment made more for fashion than warmth. Next, he worked the tight boots from her feet, his frown deepening at the sight of her thin socks. He curled his fingers around her icy toes, muttering a curse.

Slowly, he scanned the rest of her. She wore a long-sleeved denim shirt tucked and belted into a pair of black jeans. A quick peek between the buttons of her shirt revealed a white lacy bra and bare skin. His breath instinctively quickened at the sight of one white, creamy mound rising above the bra cup.

No undershirt.

Shane dropped the shirt, a guilty flush heating his cheeks. What had the woman been thinking when she set out in this weather dressed like this— and with a baby? His gaze strayed to the baby, who had become brave enough to reach for Buck as he whirled madly around her. At least she had dressed the baby warmly, he conceded grudgingly. In fact, the thick snowsuit was probably making the baby uncomfortable in the warmth of the cabin.

But first things first. Shane went to his bedroom

and came back with a pair of heavy wool socks. He slipped them over the woman's small feet, then grabbed the quilt off the back of the couch and covered her with it.

He was tucking the sides around her legs when he felt her move. Freezing in place, he glanced at her face. Her eyelashes fluttered, but remained closed. She moaned and lifted a hand to her head.

Shane leaned over her, gently pulling her hand away from the injury. "Can you hear me?" He kept his voice low, figuring she must have one hell of a headache. Served her right for being foolish enough to travel in this storm.

Her thick, dark lashes fluttered again, but this time she managed to keep them open for a few seconds—long enough for Shane to note that her eyes were such a deep blue they appeared almost purple. She quickly closed them again, as if the light hurt her eyes.

"I...hear you. My head hurts." She turned her head slightly, then moaned in pain. "What's that noise?"

Shane lifted his head. "Buck! Quiet!"

Buck immediately stopped his barking, then began to lick the baby's face. She continued to giggle, clutching his fur and pulling with all her might. Shane watched a moment to make certain Buck would tolerate this innocent abuse. When he was satisfied that Buck was a marshmallow in her hands, he looked back at the woman. A frowned wrinkled the skin between her brows.

"I'll get you some aspirin," he said, getting to his feet. What more could he do? Keep her quiet and warm...she probably suffered a concussion. Hopefully, by tomorrow, the storm would play itself out and he could contact someone for her. She certainly wasn't going anywhere in the PT Cruiser.

He helped her hold the glass so she could

swallow three aspirin, then gently wiped the water from her chin. "You need to rest," he said, his voice harsher than he intended. He had no patience for fools, especially when they endangered a baby. What *had* this woman been thinking? Where was she headed?

She looked at him, her pupils so large they seemed to blend with the irises. "Wait."

Shane stilled at the tiny note of panic in her whisper. Now she would ask about the baby. Understandably, she'd be frantic.

"I....What happened?"

"You don't remember?" Shane quirked a skeptical eyebrow.

She shook her head, crying out at the pain the movement caused.

Shane held her chin with gentle, but firm fingers. "You shouldn't move around."

"I forgot," she whispered.

Her chest rose and fell in swift, agitated movements, reminding Shane of the creamy swell of her breasts beneath the denim shirt. Disgusted with his thoughts, Shane said gruffly, "You hit a tree down the road. Buck—my dog—found you."

At that moment, the baby uttered a high-pitched squeal of delight as Buck succeeded in knocking her over with his lascivious licks. *Now* she would freak and demand to see her baby so she could check every limb to her satisfaction—

But she didn't. Instead, she grabbed his sleeve and stared at him with huge, terrified eyes. Shane was surprised at the stark emotion on the woman's face. Surely she could hear the baby, know that it was all right?

Tears welled and spilled down her cheeks. She sought to control her breathing, but Shane saw it was a losing battle. He strongly suspected she was on the verge of a full-blown panic attack. "Don't worry, despite your reckless driving, your baby's all right."

"What baby?" she cried out suddenly, startling the baby, Buck, and Shane into complete silence.

"You don't re—?" Understanding hit Shane with the force of an avalanche, chilling his bones. "Just how much *do* you remember?"

Chapter Two

She didn't have to remember her past to know this was the most terrifying experience of her life. Her memory was like a blank canvas, a stark expanse of ivory without a single drop of color.

Who was she?

Where was she?

Why couldn't she remember? The fierce-looking man hovering above her had explained about the accident...*but why couldn't she remember?*

"Do I know you?" It seemed like a logical question before she asked it, but once out in the air, she felt foolish.

"No. I've never seen you before in my life."

His black eyes flickered over her, saying without words that he would have remembered, and at the same instant giving her the impression he wasn't too pleased to meet her now. She felt a jolt shoot through her heart, then the first tingling of alarm. This fear had nothing to do with her memory lapse. She didn't know him....

"I'm Shane Knox, and this is my cabin."

Now she knew his name, but he remained a stranger—an irritated stranger. Swallowing hard, she eased her head back onto the arm rest of the couch and closed her eyes. Time. She needed time to think. Maybe if she thought hard enough, she would remember something—anything. She searched hard, but it was like fumbling in a dark room for a light switch, having no idea where it might be found.

Everything remained a mystery: who she was, where she was, how she came to be here...in a cabin with a man who looked a little on the wild side. Her anxious glance darted to the baby playing on the floor with Buck. A whisper crept out of the darkness in her mind...*you failed to protect her.* Before she could grasp its meaning, the whisper slithered away. She moaned in frustration. Why did the sight of the baby and the dog trigger a voice in her head?

Finally, her tormented mind could take no more. She let the darkness pull her in once again, away from the forbidding face of the stranger.

When she awoke again, the first thing she saw was the man. Shane—yes, he'd said his name was Shane. At least there was nothing wrong with her short-term memory, she thought with relief.

Another relief was the absence of noise. All was quiet, with the exception of the fire, which crackled and popped as the man named Shane laid fuel to the flames.

She squirmed, cautiously moving her limbs to assure herself nothing was broken. An accident, he'd said. Had she sustained nothing more than a bump on the head? Obviously, for she felt no other pain.

But her head hurt like the devil.

Speaking of devils...her gaze shot once again to the man crouching before the fireplace. Firelight flickered over his bronze profile, highlighting a high cheekbone and the curve of one thick, dark brow. The rest of his face remained in shadow. His hair was short, black and straight, and the angle of his jaw bespoke tension...and anger?

She swallowed a gasp as he suddenly turned and caught her staring. Black eyes regarded her searchingly before shifting back to the fire. His voice was a low, disturbing rumble that did nothing to quell the butterflies in her stomach.

"You're awake. I was beginning to think I'd have to chance this snowstorm and take you to the hospital." He used a poker to shift the logs around, causing a shower of sparks to rush toward the chimney.

Snowstorm. She frowned and gritted her teeth, but nothing came to mind. For all she knew, it could have been spring outside.

"How's the head?"

"Better." And it was. A faint throbbing, an occasional sharp pain when she moved, but much better than the earlier pounding horror.

He rose, and her gaze followed the movement. He was a tall man, which added to his fierce look. *Dangerous*, she thought, shivering. Scoffing at her ridiculous fears, she pushed them aside. If he had wanted to harm her, he'd already had plenty of opportunity while she lay helpless.

"I've made you some tea, and I've got chicken noodle soup warming on the stove if you feel up to it."

Her stomach rebelled at the thought of food, but her parched mouth watered at the mention of tea. "Tea sounds fine, but I don't think...food doesn't sound—"

"Fine," he growled ungraciously. "I'll get the tea."

She had never felt so unwelcome in her life. At least *that* much, she knew. He left the room and came back with a tray, giving her time to push herself into a better position before setting it on her lap.

"Watch out; the tea's hot."

Heeding his warning, she picked up the cup of tea and blew gently several times before taking a sip. It was sweet and milky, but it prompted no thoughts of her likes or dislikes. She frowned, rubbing ineffectively at a stain on the inside rim with her thumb.

Shane settled in a chair by the fire, kicking one ankle over his knee. He rubbed at the stubble on his chin and watched her. "You said before that you couldn't remember anything. Is that still true?"

She nodded, feeling miserable

He sighed as if he wasn't surprised by her answer. "I'll tell you what I know and you can see if it jars your memory, okay?"

Again she nodded. Anticipation and fear warred inside her. What if she still didn't remember anything? What then? What if she *never* remembered anything?

"Don't think about it," he ordered swiftly. "It'll just make things worse." When he seemed satisfied that he'd curtailed the hysteria he'd obviously read in her eyes, he continued. "You were driving a PT Cruiser with Texas license plates." Pausing, he watched her intently, but she could only shrug. "I found the registration papers in the glove compartment, and they say the Cruiser is registered to a Brandon Lynch."

Her fingers tightened around the cup. She waited an eternity for her mind to open up, but nothing happened. The name should mean something to her, she knew. She'd been driving the PT Cruiser, so it stood to reason she would know the name. In fact, it was likely someone very close to her. But the name meant nothing at all.

"I take it you don't recognize the name?"

"No. I don't." Her tone came out a little sharp, due to her own frustration. "It's like I've never heard that name before." Which, of course, couldn't be true unless she'd stolen the vehicle. Impossible...she didn't *feel* like a thief.

Which meant absolutely nothing at this point, because at this point, she could be anything, anyone.

"What about a purse?" All women carried purses, didn't they? Her heartbeat accelerated at the thought, but the man—Shane—dashed her hopes.

"No identification other than the registration

papers, I'm afraid. I haven't searched the area yet, so it's possible—though not likely—that your purse fell out when I opened the door. When the snow lets up, I'll take a look around."

"Meanwhile...?"

"Meanwhile, you'll have to stay here."

Again, she got the impression he wished otherwise.

"Nobody's going anywhere in this storm. I wouldn't be surprised if they've closed the interstate until the snow plows can get through."

Which prompted her next question. "Where, exactly, am I?" She had no clue. Alaska, Maine, Canada—

"North Carolina. Smokey Mountains. My guess is you were headed to Asheville, or beyond."

A baby's abrupt, disgruntled cry startled her so badly she nearly toppled the tray on her lap. Following the cry came the barking of a dog. Her wide, questioning gaze flew to his.

"She's awake." He stood, looked at her intently, then disappeared through another doorway to the right of the couch.

Moments later, while she sat frozen on the couch, he returned with a chubby toddler in his arms and a good-sized dog of an indistinguishable breed trotting at his side.

It was a beautiful baby, with dark hair and eyes, and rosy cheeks that radiated good health.

He moved the tray and gently deposited the baby on her quilt-covered lap. Automatically, her hands closed around the baby's legs to steady it. Dressed in a pink denim jumpsuit, the baby looked to be around twelve months of age.

Woman and child regarded each other in silence. The baby grinned, revealing four shiny teeth, and opened her arms.

"Gleeeeee!" the baby chortled happily, grabbing

a painful hold on her short hair and tugging hard. Shane reached over and gently disconnected her fingers.

Laughing shakily, she said, "Well, she isn't bashful, is she?"

"You should know."

She stilled. The skeptical look was back in his eyes. Both Shane and the baby possessed dark hair and eyes, so naturally she had assumed this beautiful child was....

And then she remembered his earlier reassurances about her baby being all right. Swallowing, she croaked, "You mean—this is—"

"She came with you."

****

Shane had been counting on this last trump card, but now that it had been played, his worst fears were confirmed. Unless she was an excellent actress, the woman suffered from amnesia, something he'd read about, watched on television, but had never encountered.

She didn't even recognize her own baby.

There was a wedding band on her finger, and no other logical explanation that Shane could think of for a woman traveling alone with a baby. The little girl had to belong to her.

Shock paled the woman's face. Her mouth gaped open, then fluttered closed.

Shane felt a stab of sympathy, but immediately squashed it. He had problems of his own to sort out, and this woman wasn't about to become one of them. Besides, she'd brought this on herself by driving in a snowstorm.

"I think her name is Molly," he offered, stroking the baby's soft cheek. Molly turned and clamped her tiny baby teeth onto his index finger, grinning all the while. Prudently, Shane withdrew his finger while it was still connected to his hand. "In the back

19

of the PT Cruiser, I found a suitcase filled with baby clothes. There was a T-shirt with her name on it."

"Molly."

Shane watched her whisper the name, read the helpless horror in her eyes. "Don't press it. I think— I read somewhere that it only makes it harder to remember." He paused to let that sink in before he added, "There was another suitcase with clothes."

She swung her hopeful gaze to his. "Was there— "

"No, there was no T-shirt with *your* name on it. But Molly here might have given us a clue when she first saw you. She said 'Glee', or something like that. Could mean Glynis, Glenda, Lee . , ." He stopped as something flickered in her eyes. "Do any of those ring a bell?"

She drew her brows together in fierce concentration. "Maybe. When you said, 'Lee', I felt a jolt, but I can't be certain."

"Well, we've got to call you something, so Lee it is." He glanced at Molly, who had been silently watching the exchange. "What do you think, Molly, is her name Lee?"

"Gleeeee!" Molly clapped her hands together and grinned. Drool ran down her chin and Lee automatically reached out and wiped it off with the heel of her palm.

Their gazes met; his smug, hers startled.

"See, you haven't forgotten your maternal instincts. The rest will come; you'll see." He looked away from her frightened eyes, unwilling—no, *unable* to allow himself to feel sympathy. "I also found a box filled with baby goods—a few cans of formula, baby food, a baby dish, things like that. Looks like you packed for a long trip."

Molly became restless, reaching for the big red dog waiting patiently beside the couch. "Dock! Dock!" She grunted at the restriction of Lee's hands and reached her fat little fingers out to the dog.

Shane couldn't decide whether she was trying to say 'dog', or 'Buck'. It sounded suspiciously like a combination of both. He took Molly from the woman and put her on the floor, waiting until she was steady before letting her go. From the corner of his eye, he saw that Lee eyed the dog warily.

"Don't worry; Buck loves her. In fact, you might say he saved her life." When Lee gave him a sharp look, he explained, "I didn't see her at first, but Buck wouldn't leave the PT Cruiser until I looked inside. That's when I found her in the back seat." His statement generated nothing; her expression remained blank. "Don't worry. I'm sure it will come back to you."

"Yes...I'm sure you're right."

The trembling sound of her voice told Shane she was very afraid he was wrong. And what if he was? What would he do with her—them? He'd be forced to take her to the hospital and leave her and Molly in their competent care. He'd have to walk away without ever knowing who she really was. Exactly what he needed to do. He was up here to meditate—get his head on straight—not to play hero to a foolish woman and her baby.

Keeping his attention on the happy duo on the floor, he resumed his seat and placed his arms on his knees. His angry gaze finally settled on the pale woman lying on the couch. She clutched the covers, kneading the old material with nervous fingers as she watched him watching her.

She was afraid of him. The realization bolted through Shane and he nearly laughed at it's absurdity. Did he look that dangerous? He rubbed at the two-day old stubble on his chin, suspecting he not only needed to shave, but needed a haircut as well. "I'm not a gangster; I'm a cop, so you can stop looking at me like I'm going to jump your—strangle you."

She lowered her gaze, but continued to mangle the quilt.

Shane mentally thrashed himself. It wasn't her fault his life and career were in shambles. "I'm sorry, it's just that you looked so ridiculously frightened—"

Suddenly, her violet eyes flashed up at him, giving Shane insight into the woman she was, whether she knew it or not. Lee Doe—whoever she was—was a fighter.

"Wouldn't you be, in my position? To wake up and find yourself without a memory, in a cabin alone with a—a man? Not knowing where you are, who you are, or how you got here?" She flung back the quilt and sat up, clutching her head between her palms. Tears fell on her pale cheeks and plopped onto her jeans. "I don't even recognize my own baby!"

Shane cursed to himself again and moved to sit beside her. Hesitantly, he placed his hand on her shoulder and eased her back. She went willingly with a moan and a shudder, no doubt suffering because of her outburst. "We'll figure this thing out together, okay? Just relax, let your mind rest. Buck and I will take care of Molly until you get better." Shane didn't add that he didn't know much more than Buck about how to take care of a baby.

Still, how hard could it be?

She'd closed her eyes again and appeared to be sleeping. Shane was glad, because something about this woman put him on edge—made him tense. Made him feel emotions that had always gotten him into trouble in the past.

Buck and Molly played a rousing game of tag around the living room—with Buck doing most of the running. Molly, Shane determined, hadn't yet mastered the art of walking. But she could get around quickly by crawling, keeping Buck on the move.

Shane leaned against the fireplace and surveyed the articles he'd brought in from the PT Cruiser. Bringing only the stuff he thought she and the baby would need, he'd stacked them in a corner by the door. His gaze narrowed thoughtfully. The woman— *Lee*—he reminded himself, had been traveling fully prepared. His search of the Cruiser had not only uncovered food and formula, two suitcases, a make-up case, and an opened bag of disposable diapers, but a portable high chair and baby walker as well.

He straightened abruptly. Was she moving to another state, perhaps? The articles would indicate moving, or at least an extended stay. Which meant someone would be expecting her, wouldn't they? When she didn't show up, they would start searching for her.

Perhaps she and her husband had been traveling in separate vehicles, and he was at this moment backtracking to find her.

Or...perhaps she was running from her husband, which would explain the fact that she didn't have a smidgen of identification. Maybe they'd had a fight and she'd forgotten her purse because she'd been so flustered.

Or scared.

Yeah, you'd like that scenario, wouldn't you Shane? Shane growled at his conscience, denying the accusation. He liked his solitude, liked his single status. She was a stranger—with a baby! His interest extended no further than the mystery surrounding her. No one knew better than him that a runaway was the *last* thing he needed.

"Walp! Walp, Gleeeee!"

Molly's plaintive cries gained Shane's instant attention. He jerked and swung around to find Molly pulling at the folded baby walker while balancing her chubby body against the wall.

"Walp!" She stared at him, one fist clutching the

leg of the walker, her bottom lip thrust forward in a pout. "Walp, Gleeee!"

Shane's smile wavered. The baby was staring straight at him when she wailed, "Gleee!" Was everyone Glee to the child? So much for thinking they had solved the puzzle of Lee's name. He sighed, deciding to keep this bit of news to himself. Despite the resentment he felt at having her here, Lee needed that tiny anchor.

"I'm coming, your majesty. Hang on." The closer he got to Molly and the dancing Buck, the more excited the duo became. Buck seemed to know what Shane was about to do. Molly obviously did, for she squealed and nearly unbalanced herself in her excitement.

Shane reached out and caught her as her body spun around, lifting her easily into the walker. When her feet touched the floor, she took off after Buck, guiding the walker with eerie precision. Buck scrambled backward to escape this new and faster Molly, the surprised look on his face making Shane forget himself for a moment.

He laughed out loud, the sound startling him.

Molly joined him, shrieking in uncontrollable merriment. She had trapped Buck in the corner.

His laughter faded along with his silly grin as he reminded himself that the warm feeling in his gut was only temporary. Molly belonged to someone else.

And quite possibly, so did Lee.

Which was wonderful, he told himself. *Wonderful.* Soon, someone would come to take her off his hands and he could get back to the business of sorting out his sorry life.

Hadn't he learned his lesson? There wasn't a woman on earth who understood him, or could tolerate his dedication to his job.

None.

Chapter Three

Shane watched with increasing irritation as his unexpected house guest arranged the grilled cheese triangles on the saucer until the corners matched precisely. Finally, she picked up her spoon, but instead of plunging into the steaming soup, she pushed the noodles away from the sides of the bowl until every last one was submerged in chicken broth. Several spoon-clicking moments later, she brought a spoonful of soup to her lips and blew gently. Three times exactly. Just like before with the tea.

Something queer lurched in Shane's gut. It was the same something he'd felt when watching her cool the tea earlier, but he had yet to fathom the cause. Who was this mystery woman? His gaze fell to the ring on her hand. No need to guess; it was obvious she was married. Of course, it made no difference to him either way. He wasn't interested.

"Glee! Eat! Gleeeeeeeeeee!"

He shook his head, giving in to Molly's demand for a portion of his grilled cheese sandwich. He and Lee sat at the little table in the kitchen across from each other with Molly safely ensconced between them in her high chair. He'd failed to entice Molly with several varieties of baby food; she insisted on eating the same food as them.

"Glee! Eat, eat!"

Loudly and *very* insistently. A sucker for a messy face, he speared a noodle with his fork, blew on it, then placed it on her tray alongside the now squashed piece of grilled cheese sandwich.

Strangely, she didn't eat the food; she played

with it. Shane eyed the string of noodle hanging from her matted, broth-soaked hair with faint disgust. Why did babies play with their food? Did they enjoy getting themselves all messy? Was this a type of ritual only babies understood?

Lee didn't seem to have a clue. She smiled often at the baby—winsome, sometimes tortured smiles—but offered no smug, motherly advice.

Questions with no answers. Again. His gaze returned to the woman seated opposite him, eating her soup with a dainty precision that made him feel like a backwoods hillbilly.

Two females in his hideaway and he knew nothing about either of them with the exception of their first names, and that one was a slob and the other possessed the makings of a snob.

Suddenly, he knew who Lee reminded him of with her dainty, precise mannerisms: his ex-wife. Swallowing a growl of disgust, he cleared his throat instead, uncomfortable with the silence—broken only by occasional demands from Molly as she banged the spoon she'd confiscated from Shane onto her tray. "How's your soup?" She couldn't know that she reminded him of someone he'd rather forget.

Lee swallowed her food, placed her spoon in the bowl, then carefully wiped her mouth before answering. Shane's dread deepened. The more he learned about this woman with her fragile features and pale complexion, the more she reminded him of *her*, the woman who had promised to love till death do us part.

The woman with no staying power.

"You know, it tastes suspiciously like chicken noodle."

She said this with such a serious expression on her face that it took Shane a full moment to realize she joked. His frown wavered into a stiff smile. "Well," he drawled with a hint of sarcasm, "At least we know you've got a sense of humor."

A tremulous smile revealed small, even teeth. "With this face, how could I not?"

Shane's brow rose. "I don't understand." He didn't. She possessed a heart-shaped face, with a delicate bone structure and wide-set eyes. A beautiful, interesting face. Surely she knew it. Suspecting she was fishing for compliments but taking the bait anyway, he asked, "You don't like your face?"

She grimaced, then shrugged. "Not really. Too plain. And I hate freckles."

"You do?" This was interesting, Shane thought. Expressing a dislike could mean she was beginning to remember. The faster she remembered, the sooner he could call someone and get her out of here. "I don't see anything wrong with freckles. In fact, I think they add character."

"Character?" She made a face. "Freckles are a woman's nightmare. People tend to view women with freckles as childish, irresponsible. They aren't taken seriously. *I'm* not about to give people that advantage..."

She trailed off, leaving Shane waiting in expectant silence. "Go ahead. Maybe we've stumbled upon a clue." *And I can be rid of you—you're too distracting.* He leaned forward, studying her intently, from the top of her shiny hair to the short, manicured fingernails. "Sounds like you might work in a profession where you constantly have to prove yourself. You were beginning to sound a little defensive."

"I'm sorry." Her brows came together. "I don't know where that came from."

"Don't be sorry. I can think of a few positions that might jolt your memory. An executive, a manager, a lawyer—"

"I don't think I fit any of those images." Her

little laugh was self-depreciating. "Especially not a lawyer."

Shane lifted a brow at her positive tone. "Well, I don't blame you for not *wanting* to be a lawyer— believe me, I have no respect for them myself—but your adamant reaction could indicate—"

"I'm fairly certain."

Shane stared at her clenched hands. A chill tingled down his spine. Her protest, the fact that she was so certain she wasn't when she didn't know anything else about herself...If she was a lawyer, then he'd *have* to chance the snowstorm, because he damned sure wasn't sharing his space with one!

No matter how pleasant she was to look at.

Then again, other than her comment, her tone and actions just didn't click with the image. He stared at her denim shirt, the pocket embroidered with a popular, but low-priced brand name. If she was a lawyer, then he was Daniel Boone. And he had to agree with her assessment; he couldn't imagine anyone looking less like a lawyer than the pint-size woman seated across the table. *Bet she'd like to hear that.*

Her gaze followed his to where he stared at her clothing. She waved her hands in a downward gesture, indicating her practical outfit. "There's another thing. I don't think these are my clothes."

In his surprise, Shane dropped the spoonful of noodles he was transferring onto Molly's tray. They landed on the hardwood floor with a wet plopping sound, much to Molly's delight. Scrambling on all fours, Shane began to chase the errant noodles while Molly leaned over in her high chair and dropped food onto his back. Finally, he gave up and let Buck clean up the mess—which was what he should have done in the first place. And he would have, if Lee hadn't been sitting across from him, imitating a princess.

Without denim, he would go naked. And judging

by the clothes in her suitcase, so would Lee Doe. As a matter of fact, he recalled that Molly's wardrobe contained several miniature *denim* outfits, along with a tiny set of cowboy boots.

Lawyers wore power suits and polo shirts.

Wishful thinking?

As Molly began to beat steadily on the tray with the spoon, Shane shook the food from his back and struggled with his temper—which she'd inadvertently aroused. "What are you suggesting? That someone traded suitcases with you—and they just happened to be your size?" He pretended a puzzled expression, edged with mockery, raising his voice to be heard over Molly's musical disaster with the spoon. "Oh, and they just happened to have a little girl about the size of Molly, too?"

"I don't know!"

Molly added an ear-splitting, off-beat hum to the clanging.

Shane started to speak, then realized they were both having to shout above the noise. Casting an exasperated glance at Molly, he asked instead, almost desperately, "Why is she doing that?"

Lee's response was automatic and startling. "She always does that when she wants down."

****

A shriek, a splash, muffled cursing, and a baby's high-pitched giggle were the only sounds inside the cabin. Outside the cabin, the wind howled like a banshee, and icy snow pelted the windows.

Following Shane's terse orders, Lee sat before the fire with her knees drawn tightly to her chest while Shane bathed Molly in the big claw foot tub. She hadn't considered doing the chore herself. How could she, when she didn't remember *how* to bathe a baby? What if she inadvertently harmed Molly?

But then, judging by the grim, nervous look on Shane's face, he wasn't feeling too confident about the chore, either. However, there wasn't a bit of doubt it *had* to be done.

Molly was nearly unrecognizable.

Lee sniffled and turned her other cheek to the warm fire, hoping her tears would dry before Shane noticed. Her head still throbbed, but she'd taken three aspirin a few moments ago and already the pounding had begun to fade.

What was she going to do? What if she remained in this void the rest of her life? What if she never remembered who she was, where she lived? The worst thing—and she could hardly bear to think of it—was that she couldn't remember Molly. Even after she'd blurted out that Molly wanted down from the high chair, she still didn't know where the thought had come from, or why she'd said it.

Just as she didn't know why she was so certain she wasn't a lawyer, or an executive. How had she known? Or was it something her mind refused to remember? Try as she might, she couldn't think of a reason for being so certain.

Which meant it probably wasn't true.

Don't worry, he'd said, *it'll come to you.* Lee moaned softly, choking down another sob. She suspected he'd only said those things to reassure her, because he couldn't possibly know. And why would she think these clothes didn't belong to her?

Slowly, Lee lifted her head and stared into the flames as an alarming thought came to her. What if...what if Shane Knox was lying to her? What if he *knew* who she was, but didn't want her to know? He could be a kidnapper, and she could be someone wealthy, someone with a husband willing to pay a king's ransom to get her and Molly back.

He hadn't bothered to hide his impatience over their unexpected visit. Maybe it wasn't impatience, after all. Maybe it was his nature—the nature of a criminal. He'd said he was a cop, but he could be lying.

Maybe...maybe it was just a stroke of luck that she'd hit her head and lost her memory. Or maybe *Shane* was the culprit behind the tender bump on her head. He might have delivered the blow himself.

Lee bit her lip as each possibility grew more alarming. Shane Knox could be a madman for all she really knew.

"I managed the diaper, but I need some help with these pajamas."

She jumped and swung around, making her head spin and throb. Her pulse fluttered wildly. Shane stood by the couch, holding a squirming Molly in place on the cushions with one hand. In the other, he held a piece of clothing. The frustration on his face told her he was completely out of his element.

Cautiously, she got to her feet and approached the couch. "I'm not sure...."

"Try. Please." It was an order.

She took the clothing and held it up, then began to dress the baby. Molly stared intently at her while she completed the task without faltering. Lee felt a rush of triumph as she closed the last snap and lifted Molly in her arms. She inhaled the wonderful baby smells of soap and powder, mentally willing her memory to return.

"I'll take it from here," Shane said, reaching for Molly without taking his gaze from Lee's face.

But Molly frowned at him, batting at his arms with a chubby hand. "Glee," she announced, yawning and laying her head on Lee's shoulder. Dark eyelashes swept her flushed cheeks as her eyelids drifted shut.

Lee smiled at Shane's disgruntled look. She even managed a chuckle at the sight of his drenched shirt and jeans. He looked as if he'd joined Molly in the tub fully clothed. "I'd better put her to bed. I think I can manage."

"You and Molly will sleep in my bed. I'll take the couch."

Another order, ungraciously given. Lee didn't argue, knowing it was the most logical thing to do. Poor Molly, she thought, at the mercy of two strangers. One without a memory and the other bearing the disposition of Scrooge.

Shane followed, lowering his voice. "I've put a few extra blankets on one side so Molly won't fall off."

Lee nodded, warmed by his thoughtfulness. Had she really considered him dangerous? Gruff, maybe. Dangerous—no.

"Maybe you should leave the small light on in case she wakes up in the middle of the night." He rushed around her and turned back several layers of quilts. Lee placed the sleeping baby on the sheets and tucked the covers around her. For a long moment, she stared at Molly, wondering how she could have forgotten something so precious. It didn't seem possible.

"The kerosene heater will keep it pretty warm in here." Shane pointed to a small heater in the corner of the room.

"Thank you." Lee watched as he took one last look at Molly before leaving the room. Had she imagined the painful longing in his expression? She frowned, grabbing a brightly striped pair of flannel pajamas from the suitcase. And why wasn't an attractive man like Shane Knox married? He seemed to have a way with kids.

Attractive...yes, Shane was attractive in a very basic, primitive way that struck a baffling cord inside her. Lee fastened the buttons on the pajama top, her mind running in circles. Which was she? The woman who didn't feel comfortable in denim, or the woman who could be attracted to a reclusive mountain man like Shane Knox?

Nothing made sense.

Lee paused in dressing as another thought struck her. What made her think Shane *wasn't* married? He hadn't said. In fact, there were many things she didn't know about him, yet here she was preparing to sleep under the same roof—alone, with him.

In his bed.

She didn't have a choice. A blizzard raged outside, and she didn't know who she was. *She* could be married—most likely was, if the gold wedding band on her finger was any indication.

But she could at least find out who *he* was. He'd said he was a cop. If he was, then why the isolation? Why wasn't he working? She had instinctively sensed he was unhappy about something, but what? Suddenly, she was very curious to know more about her rescuer.

Having made the decision, Lee arranged her pillows along Molly's right side, forming a barrier around the sleeping baby. She supposed mothering was much like swimming; a person never forgot.

Like making love. *You're losing it, Lee, or whoever you are.* Lee laughed without humor at the thought. Lose it? She'd obviously already lost it. Her memory, her life, and her child.

And a husband?

Silently, she tiptoed to the door and eased it open, catching Shane in the process of changing out of his wet clothes.

Stifling a gasp of embarrassment, Lee started to close the door again. She hesitated, her curious gaze drawn to the sight of his bare back.

She couldn't resist.

Her breath quickened as she watched his muscles ripple in the firelight. He slung the shirt onto the couch and turned slightly to reach for another, flinging a lock of hair from his eyes as he straightened. For a moment, she saw the tight, washboard stomach and narrow waist above his low-slung jeans before he turned his back to her again. He pulled the shirt over his head and shucked his jeans in one continuing motion, revealing rock-hard buttocks encased in white cotton underwear. His thighs looked powerful and just as hard, dusted with fine black hair.

Lee swallowed, feeling her nipples tighten in response. She didn't want him to put on another pair of jeans, as he was doing now. She wanted him to turn around. She wanted to see—

"You can come in now," he announced in a low voice. "Unless you'd like me to repeat the process so you can catch another look."

A wave of fire swept her from head to toe. Lee gripped the doorway and thought about slamming it shut, pretending she hadn't just been caught watching him undress.

But pretending wouldn't work because he knew—had probably known all along.

Slowly, she edged into the living room, glad, so very glad he had turned the lamps out. The only light came from the brightly burning fire.

"I..." Nervously, she cleared her throat. "I just needed a drink of water." A lame excuse, but the only one she could pluck out of her dazed mind.

He turned and her gaze dropped without her permission to the top button of his jeans, left carelessly undone. Of course, he wouldn't want to be uncomfortable while he slept. This logical thought prompted another; did he sleep in the raw when he was alone? She gulped at the image the possibility evoked.

"Don't be embarrassed. I should have changed in the bathroom, but I didn't want to wake Molly." He shot her a lazy, knowing smile that made Lee want to throw something at him.

But there was something else there—something besides anger at his deliberate cruelty. A rise in body temperature, illicit thoughts, and a yearning that made her stifle a tiny gasp.

Her throat felt dry, and she thought desperately that she really did need that drink.

How could she react this way to a perfect stranger?

Shane disappeared into the kitchen and returned with a glass of water. He offered it to her, the smile gone, his face shadowed and a little frightening. When she took the glass, he led the way into the living room. She followed, sinking into the chair while he sat on the sofa. Without conscious thought, she propped her feet on the edge of the cushion and wrapped her arms around her knees.

He wouldn't harm her or Molly—she sensed it— yet her imagination, devoid of anything else to remember and fret about, kept plaguing her with sinister hints and possibilities. What was a man like Shane doing in a cabin in the mountains? Was he working undercover? On vacation? Lying to her about being a cop?

There wasn't any doubt he looked dangerous. Yet, when he was around Molly, he was like a totally different man. She could easily picture him hoisting his own kids high in the air.

But now, without the buffer of Molly between them...

She cleared her throat. He folded his arms over his chest, staring at her as if waiting for her to speak. Lee set the glass of untouched water down on the table beside the chair, forcing herself to look at him. "I haven't thanked you for rescuing me," she said, her voice wavering nervously. "And Molly."

He shrugged it off. "Anyone would have done the same."

Silence fell. Lee fidgeted. Finally, she slid her

gaze to the fire, unable to maintain the steady eye-contact. She felt shaken, scared, and far too curious for her own good.

"You're nervous."

Too hastily, she shook her head, but didn't answer. The lie came easier without speaking. And she didn't fool him at all.

"Yes, you are. Why, I wonder? If I wanted to...murder you, or worse --" He slanted her a mysterious look she was sure was meant to scare. "Then I would have done it already, don't you think?"

Lee decided to give up trying to deny the obvious and ran her tongue over her dry lips. She *was* frightened, and this brute seemed to enjoy it. Staring at his face, she watched the play of firelight over his smooth, bronze features. She couldn't imagine this man being afraid. It must be nice. But then, he didn't have *her* problems, either. "It's scary, not remembering anything." Just as it was scary, being here with him. Isolated. Cut off from the outside world. Nobody to hear her cry for help.

"Maybe you don't want to."

His blunt statement hung in the air between them. Lee slowly uncurled her legs, disbelief momentarily robbing her of speech. Finally, she sputtered, "That's crazy. Why wouldn't I want to remember who I am?" She'd never given a thought to the possibility, and didn't now, because she desperately wanted to remember.

Didn't she? Of course she did! Now he was making her doubt her own mind just when she was beginning to find some kind of balance.

Shane seemed unperturbed by her volatile reaction. He moved from the couch to poke at the fire, his gaze narrowed against the blaze. "It was just a thought. I've read that when someone suffers from amnesia after going through a traumatic experience they'd rather forget, sometimes they're slower to recover their memory."

"And you think that could have happened to me?" she whispered, dismayed by the thought. Irrational guilt swamped her. Molly....How could someone not want to remember Molly? Lee shook her head. No, that couldn't possibly be the case. She told him so, too. "No, I'm positive I could never be that terrible a mother—to want to forget my own child!"

He crouched before the fire, his gaze intent, watchful.

Hard.

"I'm not implying you would forget on purpose, Lee. And it's not Molly I'm thinking you want to forget."

"Then...who? What?" Lee feared his words without having a clue what he was going to say. It was all just speculation on his part, she reminded herself. The reminder didn't help.

"A husband or boyfriend, maybe." He rose and placed another log on the fire, his movements lithe and as silent as a panther on the prowl. Finally, he braced his arm against the mantle and sighed. "Why else would you be traveling alone with a small child—so far from home?"

Lee stiffened, unable to let his sexist remark go unchallenged. To hell with not knowing him. "Vacation, possibly? And lots of single women have babies these days, or haven't you noticed? Do you honestly think they're all too afraid to travel alone? I just might be one of those brave, adventurous women who *isn't* afraid."

Right now, she didn't feel brave; she felt foolish for having such a silly argument with a stranger whose temperament she didn't know. *You're too impulsive...*

The condemning, inner voice stopped the

moment she noticed its appearance inside her head. Lee gripped the armchair with both hands, her eyes going wide as she tried to hold onto the memory. "I think I just—I might have remembered something," she whispered, feeling dizzy and slightly nauseous.

Shane straightened from the mantle, his expression instantly alert. "What?"

Lee closed her eyes and bit down on her tongue. The voice hadn't belonged to her, she was certain. It was a male voice, and definitely unpleasant. But no matter how hard she tried, she couldn't remember anything else. "I'm not sure." She hesitated. "It could have been something I heard on the radio, or watched on television." She gave a shaky laugh. "It sounded like a line from a soap opera."

Big, warm hands landed on her knees. Startled by the sudden contact, Lee jumped and opened her eyes. He'd moved so soundlessly she hadn't heard him, and now he knelt before her, his black, fathomless eyes inches from her own. His fingers flexed, prickling her skin beneath the flannel and making her fully aware of his touch.

"Tell me," he urged, his gaze boring into hers.

Dry-mouthed, Lee said, "The voice inside my head said I was impulsive." Her lips quirked in a fleeting, half-hearted smile. "See, I told you it wasn't much. And I don't think it was talking about me, because I don't *feel* like the impulsive type."

For a long, breathless moment, Shane stared at her. His eyes darkened. Lee sucked in a stunned breath, sensing the attraction crackling between them, both alarmed and elated.

Then he slowly moved in, bringing his face closer. "There's one way to find out."

Before she could guess his intention, his mouth moved over hers in a kiss that shattered the world around her and filled her mind with impossible questions. One stood out among the others: why did this feel like home?

Chapter Four

Shane knew he'd made a mistake the moment his mouth touched hers. Warm, soft, and supple...her mouth was every man's dream, and kissing her surpassed any fantasy he'd ever had, both as an adult and an adolescent.

Kissing her was magic, evoking a burst of desire so fierce he felt it like a physical punch in the gut.

And it scared the absolute hell out of him.

He jerked back, his stunned expression mirrored in her eyes. Whatever it was, he realized she had felt it too.

The knowledge deepened his fear, and Shane hated fear. He hated seeing it in other people, just as he hated experiencing it.

So he did what came naturally to him; he fought it.

He settled back on his heels with his hands firmly on his knees, staring at her as he decided the best excuse for what he'd just done. It would have to be something good, he thought, wondering if his blood would ever cool. Damn, but she was beautiful...fragile, and sexy. *What a combination,* his conscience taunted him sarcastically. Especially the *fragile* part, considering his penchant for damsels in distress.

Shane ground his teeth, hoping she'd keep her huge, doe-like eyes focused above his waist until he regained control of his body. When she lifted her fingers to her lips, Shane saw they were trembling. He muttered a curse beneath his breath, believing he'd frightened her.

"Why—why did you do that?" she asked in a whisper.

A whisper without fear, Shane thought with relief. Now to give her an answer that not only protected his emotions, but explained away his own impulsive behavior.

"Just testing you to see if you *are* impulsive," he said with a light shrug.

"And?"

"What do *you* think?" Shane countered, resisting the urge to touch her again. "Does kissing me ring any bells?"

"It rings a *lot* of bells." Her furious blushing told Shane she hadn't meant to voice her confession. "I mean, obviously I've kissed a man before."

Her spontaneous admission sent a burst of warmth straight to his heart—and a ball of flame straight to his groin. He frowned to compensate for the unwanted reaction. His gaze fell on her hand where the gold wedding ring glinted in the firelight. "Obviously," he murmured. "We already knew that much."

She twisted the ring, her movements revealing her agitation. "I don't feel married. In fact, I can't imagine responding to you...the way I did if I were married." Her eyes clouded with confusion. She put a hand to her head and began to rub her forehead. "It just doesn't make sense! You'd think I would feel guilty or something. Instead..."

Shane didn't realize he was holding his breath until his lungs began to burn. A part of him wanted her to finish her statement; another part of him was glad when she didn't.

With an inward sigh, he rose and returned to the fireplace, putting sensible distance between them. He'd been too long without a woman, he thought, staring into the fire. And this woman was not only attractive, she was in his cabin, eating his

41

food, warming herself by his fire...awakening his protective instincts, not to mention his libido.

If he'd met her on the street, he felt he could have easily resisted her. With her here, in his cabin, sleeping in his bed...he wasn't certain. The fact that she was obviously attracted to him as well didn't help matters.

He cleared his throat. "I apologize. I shouldn't have taken advantage of you like that." Instead of accepting his apology, she surprised him by rejecting it.

"Don't apologize. If I hadn't wanted you to kiss me, I could have stopped you."

Shane remained silent. He glanced at her quickly, saw she was picking nervously at the quilt and realized she wasn't as cool about the kiss as she wanted him to believe. He felt a perverse pleasure in the knowledge.

"Besides," she continued. "I learned something about myself, didn't I? I *can* be impulsive."

Belatedly, it occurred to Shane that she was attempting to ease his guilt over the kiss. He nearly smiled, thinking he had just learned something about her, too. She was gutsy, and unafraid to shoulder her share of the blame. It was a rare trait that Shane had always admired in people.

But he didn't want to admire this woman, he reminded himself sternly. And the very last thing he needed was to get involved with a strange woman and her baby.

A very *cute* baby named Molly, who brought out the puppy in Buck and painted herself with her food. Another day in her company and Shane knew he'd be as mushy as the food she squished between her chubby little fingers.

"You should probably get some rest," he said gruffly, keeping his eyes on the fire instead of her soft, kissable mouth. When was the last time he'd felt that type of explosive reaction from kissing a woman? He couldn't remember if he ever had, not even with his ex-wife in the early days of their marriage...before he'd found out she had another, unpleasant side to her character.

"I suppose you're right. I'll just brush my teeth then, and get to bed."

He heard her rise, heard the soft sound of her footsteps as she disappeared into the bedroom, then reemerged to go into the bathroom. She closed the door with a soft click.

The water came on, and Shane closed his eyes, his acute hearing aware of every brush stroke as he envisioned her standing at the sink, brushing that sweet, kissable mouth. The sound went on and on, so long that he glanced at his watch and frowned.

She'd been brushing her teeth for five minutes. Who in hell brushed their teeth that long? Was this another revelation, another insight into her character? He gave his shoulders a roll, telling himself there was nothing wrong with good personal hygiene habits, not even obsessive ones.

Obsessive. Shane mulled over that word, reluctant to place Lee Whoever in that category. His ex-wife had been borderline obsessive, and it had driven him insane. Well, that, and her constant harping about the long hours he worked and his dedication to his job.

He knew nothing about Lee. *She* knew nothing about herself. For all they knew, she could be mimicking the actions of another.

Shane threw a log on the fire and stepped back, forcing himself to acknowledge the possibility that Lee could also be subconsciously revealing her own personal traits.

So what? She was nothing to him. Just a stranger from the storm, with huge, beautiful eyes and a blank memory. When the storm let up, he'd take them to Asheville and leave them to the experts.

For some reason Shane couldn't explain, the thought left him empty and aching.

****

"Buck! Keep it down, buddy."

"Gleee! Uuuuck! Dadadadada!"

The noises penetrated the wall between the living area and Shane's bedroom, where Lee slept. She opened her eyes, then quickly closed them again as pain lanced through her head. It was morning, and above the baby's excited, high-pitched squeals and the gruff barking of the dog, she could hear the wind howling. Sleet pinged against the bedroom window in erratic waves.

So the storm continued, she mused. She rolled onto her back, slowly opening her eyes and staring at the ceiling.

Waiting for her mind to open up, to remember who she was, and why she was here, in this cabin, with a handsome stranger who blew hot and cold. A rugged stranger with dark, brooding eyes that revealed an inner sadness...and an intriguing mystery. She sensed that Shane Knox harbored dark secrets, and he guarded them carefully.

Who was he? Why was he here, alone in this secluded cabin?

She sighed, thinking she should be asking *herself* these questions, instead of obsessing about her host.

Obsessing. Now, why had she used that word? Wasn't it rather strong for an understandable curiosity? She was trapped in a cabin with a strange man and a baby she didn't recognize. Very understandable to be curious about Shane, just as he must be curious about her.

Lee swung the heavy covers to the side. She grimaced at the sight of her rather gaudy pajamas, then frowned over her reaction. Shane was right. Why would she have these clothes if they didn't belong to her?

Yet, her reasoning didn't explain the faint disgust she felt when she looked at them. Maybe they had been a gift, and she felt obligated to wear them. It was the best possible scenario she could imagine for *why* she wore them if she didn't like them.

She swung her feet from the bed to the floor and stood, hugging herself against the chill in the room. The pajamas might not be pretty, she thought, but they were warm and comfortable. As were the thick, men's socks she wore on her feet.

Looking down, she tried to imagine a tough and rugged man like Shane slipping socks over her feet, as he must have done when she was unconscious. She shook her head and sighed, exasperated with herself for constantly thinking about him. Padding to the door, she opened it and slipped through, coming to a halt in the doorway.

The scene before her was enough to render her momentarily speechless.

Buck ran in circles around the baby, who in turn maneuvered the walker in circles after him, laughing and squealing. Shane was crouched beside the whirling walker holding a plate filled with scrambled eggs. He held out a fork, aiming for Molly's mouth each time she passed by him.

His expression was both exasperated and amused. "Come on, Molly. Just one more bite and we'll call it quits. You've got to be hungry."

With a squeal and a scream, Molly whirled past the outstretched fork without pausing. In fact, Lee mused, her lips twitching involuntarily, the baby seemed oblivious of Shane altogether.

"Maybe she doesn't like scrambled eggs," Lee said by way of announcing her presence. When

Shane looked her way, she felt a melting sensation in her knees. She grabbed the doorway for support, startled by her reaction. Her lips tingled, as if remembering his kiss from the night before.

"Good morning," he said, his voice a little on the rough side. "Did you sleep well?"

Lee nodded, unable to look away from the liquid heat of his gaze. What was it about this man? she wondered. Was she suffering from some type of hero worship because he'd saved her life? But Lee knew it was something more. The physical attraction between them was far too strong to be categorized.

She swallowed hard as he rose and set the plate on an end table, then came toward her. He walked with the fluid grace of an animal, she thought, automatically bracing herself. Behind him, Buck and Molly continued on as if Lee and Shane were invisible.

"Let me check your head," Shane said, reaching her. Gently, he lifted her hair from the wound site and leaned close.

Her breath became short and erratic, and a hot flush infused her neck and face. Just from his nearness, she thought, trying to control her breathing.

She wasn't successful.

He let go of her hair and pulled back, frowning at her. "Are you all right? You look a little flushed." He placed a cool palm against her forehead. "But you don't feel like you have a fever."

"I'm just a little dizzy," she lied. She *was* dizzy, but she was fairly certain it had nothing to do with her injury. "Do you have any oranges?"

"Oranges?" he echoed, sticking his thumbs in his jean pockets.

"For orange juice."

"You've got to be kidding."

Lee's flush deepened as she realized how silly

she sounded. "No, I—never mind. I don't know where that came from. Of course you wouldn't have fresh oranges."

"I've got frozen," he offered. "And fresh brewed coffee."

"I don't drink coffee." Her startled gaze flew to his and held for a long moment. "At least, I don't *think* I do," she added in a strangled whisper.

Molly chose that moment to race the walker in her direction. She slammed into Lee's leg, knocking her into Shane. His arms came up and around her, and she found herself inhaling his woodsy, clean scent.

"Gleee!!!" Molly cried, pushing against the walker with all her might. "Gleee!!!"

Reluctant to leave Shane's arms, Lee pushed herself upright, looking down into Molly's drooling, smiling face. Her laugh was shaky as she said, "Well, she's certainly a cheerful baby, isn't she?" When Molly held out her arms, Lee gingerly lifted the baby from the walker. The baby's feet got tangled in the cloth seat, and Shane darted in to help untangle her.

"She drank a bottle of formula, but I haven't gotten her to eat anything else. I tried cereal, but she dumped it on the floor." Shane shook his head, looking out of his depth. "So I scrambled her an egg." He gestured to the plate. "As you can see, she isn't interested in eating."

Lee held the baby, willing her mind to remember. Molly wrapped her chubby arms around her neck and squeezed the life out of her, then planted a wet kiss on her cheek, but nothing the baby did prompted anything familiar. "You—you think I should try feeding her?" Lee asked around a lump in her throat. "If I'm her mother—"

"If?" Shane interrupted softly. "I don't think it's a question of *if*, do you? Why else would you be traveling with a baby?"

Frowning, Lee shifted the baby to her hip. "Then why doesn't she call me mama instead of Glee?"

Shane looked away, sighing. "I didn't want to mention it, but I guess I should. She calls *me* Glee, too. I don't think it has anything to do with your name."

"Oh." Lee swallowed her disappointment at this setback. "So you think she just hasn't learned to say mama?"

"That's what I'm thinking," he said reluctantly.

He had been trying to protect her feelings, she thought, and the realization warmed her. Shane Knox might give the impression of gruff impatience, but somewhere inside that rock-hard chest, there beat a heart fully capable of great kindness.

Lee sat on the couch and picked up the plate of scrambled eggs. She settled Molly on her lap and speared a fork full of eggs. Molly watched her with bright eyes, and just as Lee reached her mouth with the eggs, Molly slapped the fork with her hand.

The eggs went flying in the air, landing on the floor with a soft plop. Buck immediately pounced on the prize and gulped it down.

Molly observed the dog a moment, then clapped her hands and chortled. Before Lee could anticipate her actions, the baby leaned forward, grabbed the plate, and dumped it in the floor. Tail wagging happily, Buck began to push the upturned plate across the floor with his nose.

"I think you're right," Shane said dryly. "She doesn't care for eggs."

"At least *Buck* does." Lee looked at the baby as she yawned and rubbed her eyes. "Is she sleepy, do you think?"

"Probably. We've been up since six. It's nearly noon now."

She gave a start. "Noon? I slept until noon? I

always get up...at..." Whatever she was going to say drifted into a dense fog and was lost. She gnawed her lip in frustration. "I think I almost remembered something—"

"Don't force it," Shane warned. "It will make your head hurt."

The baby's head fell onto her shoulder and she yawned again. Lee could feel her little body relaxing as she drifted off to sleep. Without thinking, she began to rock the baby, humming beneath her breath. She was intensely aware of Shane watching her.

After a few moments, Shane reached down for the baby. "She's asleep. I'll go put her to bed."

When he returned a few moments later, he held out his hand for her to take. "Come on. You must be hungry. I'll fix us some lunch."

"Oh, I can—"

"It's no big deal."

Hesitantly, she took his hand and let him pull her to her feet. His palm was strong and warm and calloused, sending an alarming tingle along her arm. She tried to pull free, but he kept a firm grip on her as he led her into the small kitchen.

She sank onto a chair and watched him as he moved efficiently to the cupboard, then to the stove. He opened a can of soup and poured the contents into a pan, then added water.

None of his actions sparked a memory, much to her frustration. With a glum sigh, she propped her chin in her hands, breaking the silence. "Is this your permanent home?"

He stirred the soup, answering her without turning around. "No. I mostly use it during hunting season."

Not exactly a revelation, she mused, her curiosity peaking. "I guess the storm spoiled your hunting trip."

"It's not hunting season." He took out a skillet, buttered two slices of bread, and put them into the pan. "One sandwich, or two?"

"Just one, please." She chewed her thumbnail, gathering her courage. If she was going to spend time with him, then she felt justified in wanting to know more about him. Never mind the fact that she was just plain interested. "If it's not hunting season, then why are you here?"

He turned so suddenly, she jumped. His eyes were black as night, and just as unreadable. He held a spatula in one hand, and Lee saw that his knuckles had turned white where he gripped the handle. She had definitely rattled him.

"I told you I'm a cop. I'm on suspension."

"Oh." The only thing humorous about his smile, she observed, was the shape of it. Her urge to continue the same line of questioning was too strong to ignore, making her wonder about her profession— if she had one. A reporter might have the same urges, she thought with a surge of hope. "Do you mind me asking why?"

Presenting his broad back again, he flipped the sandwiches in the skillet, then stirred the soup before answering, his voice cooler by a few degrees. "As a matter of fact, I do mind. You're the one with amnesia. Let's concentrate on *your* life, shall we? How old are you?"

"I don't know."

"When is your birthday?"

"I don't know."

"Are your parents still alive?"

Lee found herself clenching her fists. "I don't know."

"Do you like pizza?"

"I don't know! Why are you—"

He slid the sandwich onto a plate and brought it to her, his eyes hard and flat. "Because one of my questions might trigger something, that's why."

"One of *my* questions might also trigger something," Lee said, growing angry at his badgering.

"And I'm a cop. Cops ask questions."

"Maybe *I'm* a cop, too," she shot back. "Maybe that's why *I* ask questions."

His bark of laughter stung. "You're not a cop, Lee."

Lee angled her chin. "What makes you so certain?"

Shane set the plate on the table, grabbed her arms, and hauled her to her feet. He used one hand to capture her hands behind her back, effectively pinning her against his chest. His eyes blazed into hers. Lee felt as if someone had pressed her full-length against the hot, hard surface of an iron. Her knees tried to buckle, and her heart leaped into her throat.

Not from fear, but from desire.

"Because if you were a cop, you would never have let me do this," Shane said, his voice oddly husky.

Unaccountably incensed, Lee narrowed her eyes at him, trying valiantly to ignore the tightening of her breasts where they touched his chest. Very softly, she asked, "Is *this* why you got suspended, Officer Knox?"

Chapter Five

He let her go so abruptly, Lee fell back into her chair. If possible, his eyes darkened further. His flushed cheeks told her she'd hit a nerve.

His low, scathing voice confirmed it. "I don't manhandle women."

"Then what do you call what you just did to me?" Maybe she should have dropped it, but Lee found she couldn't.

"I was proving to you that you aren't a cop."

"You *proved* nothing." When he simply stared at her in a smug way, Lee felt something inside her snap. She stood and closed the distance between them. Winding her arms around his neck, she stood on her tiptoes and pressed her mouth to his.

His arms came around her waist, tightened, and pulled her even closer. He deepened the unexpected kiss, moving his mouth on hers, outlining her lips with his tongue. A groan sounded low and deep in his throat.

Heat flooded Lee's belly. What had she done? His mouth was hot and demanding on hers, making her want...making her want...

Breathing hard, she pulled free and stepped out of his arms. She'd made her point, but at what cost? "You didn't stop me, and *you're* a cop," she pointed out unnecessarily. She was very satisfied to note that he was breathing hard, too. And his eyes. Oh, God, his eyes. They were pitch black and gleaming with a stark need that struck an answering chord inside of her.

The realization prompted a silent question. Why

would she feel such raw, almost savage desire if she were married? Had Shane hit on the truth when he mentioned that she might be running from a husband or a boyfriend? Was it possible she was running from an unsatisfying marriage?

"I think it would be a good idea if you didn't do that again."

Lee snapped to attention, lifting her brow, amazed and confused by her own courage. "Are you threatening me?"

"No." His gaze slid slowly, hotly, over her. "I'm just giving you fair warning." His voice lowered, deepened. "You felt too damned good, Lee. *That's* why you shouldn't tempt me."

His knee-buckling admission took the heat out of her anger. "Oh," she managed to say weakly.

"Sit down. Eat."

She obeyed his orders without question. When he set a steaming bowl of chicken noodle soup in front of her, then seated himself across from her and began to eat, she let several moments go by before she ventured, "I'm sorry. I don't know what got into me."

He flicked a brief, hot glance at her, then resumed eating.

Lee squirmed in her seat, waiting for her soup to cool. She picked up a toasted cheese triangle and took a bite. When she'd swallowed, she asked, "How—how long do you think the storm will last?"

"Hard to tell." He shrugged, drawing her attention to his broad shoulders, encased in forest green flannel. "Might be days before it lets up."

She swallowed hard at the thought of spending more days and nights in close proximity to a man as attractive and unfathomable as Shane. "You don't think we could try to make it to—"

"No," he said harshly. "I won't risk Molly's life in a storm like this."

His punishing words cut her deeply. She gasped and put a hand to her suddenly churning stomach. The edges of her vision began to gray, and a sharp pain pierced her head. Bewildered at her reaction, she gripped the table edge and tried to focus on Shane, who regarded her with astonishment.

But she couldn't focus. Her vision continued to dim until everything faded to black.

****

"Dammit!" Shane caught Lee before she hit the hardwood floor. The last thing she needed was another bump on her head. He gathered her up and strode into the living room, placing her on the couch in front of the fire.

Kneeling beside her, he smoothed the hair from her pale face, muttering every curse in his vocabulary. He'd caused her reaction, he suspected, by his harsh reminder that she had been reckless with Molly's life.

Shane frowned down at her. Could that be the reason Lee couldn't remember? Because she believed she'd been unforgivably reckless with Molly's life? He supposed it was possible. Yet...wouldn't the knowledge that Molly was okay reassure her? Allow her memory to return?

No, he decided, it had to be something more. Something deeper, more complicated. He picked up the hand wearing the wedding ring, staring at the glinting reminder that she belonged to another man.

Her eyes fluttered. She moaned and stirred, opening her eyes.

Shane found himself drowning in the stormy blue of her eyes. *There's a very lucky man out there somewhere, looking for her,* he thought before he could censure it. The reminder should have been enough to prompt Shane into keeping his hands to himself.

But it wasn't.

He cupped her pale cheek in his huge, roughened hand, offering her a genuine, apologetic smile. "I shouldn't have been so tough on you," he said gruffly.

She searched his gaze for a long, heated moment. "We know nothing about me, so you couldn't have known I was the fainting type." She offered him a wry smile and an unexpected blush. "It's not exactly flattering to find out you're a wimp."

"You're not a wimp," Shane argued with absolute conviction. "I don't think I've ever had a woman lay one on me the way you did. That took courage, considering you don't know me."

"That wasn't courage. It was stupidity." She struggled to a sitting position, then gingerly stood. "I think I should finish that soup. Maybe it was hunger that made me faint."

Shane didn't think so, but he could tell the excuse comforted her, so he let it ride.

When they were both seated again, she picked up her spoon and dug in, slurping her soup and sucking the errant noodles into her mouth as if she was a child. When she caught him watching her, she offered him a sheepish smile.

"Either I'm extremely hungry, or I'm a slob."

So she didn't remember the dainty way she'd eaten her soup the day before, Shane mused, more than a little confused over the contradiction. He shook his head, watching her peel off the crust from her grilled cheese and hand feed it to Buck.

The woman from yesterday would never have fed the dog from the table. Shane was very certain of that.

Which woman was she? The woman who sipped her soup like a lady? Or the down home woman who ate lunch in her funky striped pajamas, gave her crust to the dog and slurped her soup? Watching her was not only confusing, it was disconcerting.

Until he reminded himself that she was only temporary. In a few days, she would be driving someone else nuts.

"You asked me earlier why I was suspended," he said abruptly.

She shot him a surprised look, then cast her gaze to her soup again, chasing a noodle with her spoon. She finally used her finger to push the noodle onto her spoon. "I shouldn't have pried. You have every right to your privacy. After all, Molly and I are the ones who—"

"I got suspended because I lost my temper with a perp."

"I'm sure you had your reasons," she said graciously.

Shane noticed she didn't ask what a 'perp' meant, and filed the information away to examine later. Everything, small or great, could be a clue to her identity. Or at least her personality. He clenched his fingers around his spoon as he said, "The guy beat up his girlfriend." Her sharp intake of breath at the news gratified him. If only his captain felt the same way, he thought ruefully.

"There. You see? The guy deserved whatever you gave him."

The naivety of her declaration made him smile. "Actually, all I did was curse a blue streak at him..." He'd had better control the second time around, but it had been tricky.

"And you got suspended for *that*?" She sounded outraged on his behalf. "That doesn't sound fair. Maybe you should talk to a—" She stopped abruptly, obviously recalling his earlier sentiments about lawyers. "Someone," she supplied.

"No. Captain Maynard was right. I'm taking the job too personally." She didn't know about last year and his unforgettable run-in with Bobby Dillon, Shane thought. What would she think about him if he told her that his quick temper had cost a woman her life? But he couldn't tell her, so it didn't matter. Even now, he couldn't think about Sandra Dillon without breaking out in a cold sweat.

She set her spoon down and fed the rest of her sandwich to a grateful Buck. "I'm confused. How does taking your job personally make you a bad cop? Wouldn't that make you a *better* cop?"

He hesitated, then shook his head. "Not in this instance, no."

"Why do I get the impression you're about to leave me hanging?"

When he didn't answer, she let out a lusty sigh that sent a primitive tremor straight to his gut.

"On that note, I think I'll go check on Molly and get dressed." She made a face at her oversized PJs. "I can't wait to get out of this clown suit."

"You look—" He paused, and so did she. She waited expectantly...hopefully, Shane realized with a flicker of bewilderment. The woman acted as if she'd never received a compliment! "Sexy in those pajamas," he finished huskily.

"Sexy?" she squeaked in disbelief, then threw back her head and laughed. "What you really meant to say was that I look like an immature little girl."

He shook his head, still baffled by her conflicting reactions. One moment she waited hopefully for a compliment, and the next she was laughing in scornful disbelief when he gave her one. "Don't put words into my mouth. You don't know me."

She sobered quickly. "You're right, I don't. And we can't forget that we don't know *me*, either." Her eyelids suddenly drooped, and her expression softened.

Shane's pulse skyrocketed.

"But what I *do* know about you, Shane Knox, I like. You're a good man, and a good cop."

He watched her walk away, muttering beneath his

breath, "Don't bet the farm on that one, sweetheart." At that moment, he felt like a first-class fraud on both counts.

****

Lee stood before the bathroom mirror and stared at her reflection. Sexy. Shane had said she looked sexy in her ridiculous pajamas, and he'd sounded as if he meant it.

She frowned and quickly stripped them off, then surveyed her naked body in the mirror, looking for signs of childbirth. Either she was one of the lucky few who went through nine months of pregnancy without stretch marks, or Molly wasn't her baby.

And if Molly didn't belong to her, then to whom did she belong? Lee rubbed her aching head and squeezed her eyes tightly shut, forcing her mind to think, *think!*

The only thing she accomplished was to make her head hurt worse. She sighed and gave up, turning to her open suitcase balanced on the commode. Maybe there was something inside that would trigger a memory.

Slowly, she discarded article after article of casual clothing, mostly varying shades of denim. If she was such a denim freak, then why didn't she remember?

When she came across a calf-length, khaki skirt, she paused, eyeing the garment with one critical brow arched. The garment was better than the endless supply of jeans and western style shirts, but it still didn't quite suit her. She set it aside and rummaged through the rest of the clothes until she came across a long-sleeve, beige silk blouse that would go with the skirt. It wasn't a power suit, but—

Power suit? Lee froze, her mind helplessly trying to grasp the thought before it slipped away. With a snarl of frustration, she threw the denim clothes back into the suitcase and slammed it shut.

A half-hour later, she emerged from the bathroom immaculately dressed, her make-up flawless. No freckles in sight, no denim to be found. She felt almost human again, and definitely stronger. Were her *clothes* actually responsible for this new-found confidence? she wondered, checking on Molly and depositing her suitcase at the foot of the bed. It sounded rather shallow to think so, but she had to admit it was exactly how she felt. More confident.

Stronger.

Stronger for what? And was this really *her?* If so, then why would her entire wardrobe consist mainly of jeans and casual shirts?

Her train of thought was giving her a headache, so she switched to thinking about Shane and his suspension, and what he hadn't said. She sensed there was much more to the story, and wondered why he hadn't told her. Was he ashamed? Afraid? Guilty?

She couldn't imagine Shane Knox fearing anything. That left shame or guilt.

Possibly both, Lee thought, recalling his shadowed expression. Definitely a mystery there, and she loved unsolved mysteries—

She did? Lee paused to examine the thought. Elation filled her as she realized it was a *solid* thought. A genuine realization. A hint that her memory might be returning!

She *loved* mysteries! Such a small thing, yet she felt as if someone had just handed her a winning lottery ticket. Every tiny piece of the puzzle was to be hoarded and cherished.

Eager to share her discovery with Shane, she went in search of him. It didn't take her long to realize he wasn't in the cabin. A quick glance at the coat rack by the door, and another glance at the nearly empty firewood box told her what she needed to know.

Shane had gone out to gather more wood for the fireplace.

Her quick grasp of the situation was another small victory, and told her not only did she love solving mysteries, she was apparently fairly good at it. Of course, it didn't take a genius to figure out that Shane had gone out to gather wood. The storm continued to rage—what else would he be doing in the midst of it?

Chuckling at her own silly conceit, Lee went to the kitchen. It was only fair that she do her share of the cooking and cleaning, she decided. After all, she and Molly were uninvited guests.

A quick glance in the small, ancient refrigerator brought a frown to her brow. There was a package of cheese, a jar of mayo, a carton of eggs, and a withered head of lettuce. What was the man planning to eat during his exile? Eggs and chicken noodle soup, day in and day out? She clucked her tongue and turned to inventory the pantry.

She let out a dismayed gasp at the clutter. Wearing a grim smile, she rolled up her silk sleeves and went to work.

Lee was nearly finished when Shane spoke from behind her, making her jump.

"What in the hell are you doing?"

Slowly, she turned, her eyes going wide at his fierce frown.

It went extremely well with his growling voice.

She held a can of chicken noodle in one hand, and a can of ravioli in the other. With a helpless shrug, she used her chin to gesture to the neat rows of canned goods. "I'm, um, rearranging your pantry?"

"Like hell you are." His frown deepened as he reached out and ran a cold finger along the bridge of her nose. "What happened to your freckles?"

"I covered them with makeup."

"Why?"

"I don't know. Look, if you—"

"And what happened to your jeans? You'll freeze to death in that blouse and skirt."

Lee wasn't about to admit that she had been dodging a frigid draft from the moment she stepped out of the bathroom. Her legs felt like icicles, and her nipples had formed permanent peaks. "I'm really quite comfortable, thank you," she lied through her teeth.

As if to mock her, Shane's gaze zeroed in on her plainly visible, hardened nipples. "If that's the case, I guess I can assume you're happy to see me?"

She gasped. "Don't be crude!"

Shane's gaze snapped to her outraged face, not bothering to hide his surprise. "Crude? *I'm* not the one standing in the kitchen wearing a see-through blouse in the middle of a freezing snowstorm." He stepped closer. "If you were trying to get my attention, it worked."

"I wasn't trying to get your attention," she denied hotly, backing up until her spine connected with the pantry door behind her. There was something shivery and primitive in the look he was giving her. It made her belly quiver and her breasts tighten in response. She licked her lips, then wished she hadn't when his gaze focused on her mouth. "I— I just wanted to wear something a little more sophisticated. I don't like jeans."

Softly, he drawled, "You might not like them, but they damned sure like *you*."

"Shane—"

"Say it again."

"What?"

"Say my name again," he ordered huskily, inching closer and closer to her mouth. He braced a hand above her head, muttering an indistinguishable curse beneath his breath.

Lee slumped against the door, her knees going weak at the blatant desire on his face. She took a deep, shaky breath, causing her breasts to swell and touch his chest.

She quickly exhaled, but not before she felt the heat of his body sear her nipples with fire. Why was she fighting it, anyway? This attraction—this body chemistry—was too strong to fight, wasn't it? And why should she? There was a ring on her finger, true, but no memory of a husband.

Didn't that leave her conscience free and clear?

"Shane..." Lee whispered, and this time, she gave free rein to her desire, let it thicken her voice to match his. Her breath quickened as his warm lips settled gently on hers, teasing, nibbling, tormenting her. She curled her arms around his neck and pulled him forcibly toward her in the hopes of deepening the kiss.

A muffled thump followed by a baby's sharp cry effectively doused the inferno.

Shane jerked back, looking dazed and startled.

"Molly!" Lee breathed, sounding as horrified as she felt. As Shane turned to run, she stumbled after him, fear smothering the last lingering fog of desire.

Chapter Six

"She looks okay," Shane said with heartfelt relief after he'd examined the now whimpering baby. He had to repeatedly push Buck out of the way.

"Let me see." Lee went over old territory, turning Molly this way and that. "I can't find any marks or bumps."

"I really think she's okay."

"I should have been paying attention—"

"The pillows were in place," Shane reminded her, wishing he could erase that awful look of self-condemnation in her eyes. "Unless one of us stays with her every time she sleeps, there's always the possibility she could fall from the bed."

"Then I should have stayed. I'm her mother."

"Stop blaming yourself." When she stared pointedly at him, he flushed. Obviously he wasn't doing a very thorough job of hiding his *own* guilt. He sighed and ran a hand through his hair, wondering ruefully if he'd acquired any gray ones since finding his new houseguests yesterday morning.

Lee held the baby close, murmuring apologies over and over again as she rained kisses on the baby's tear-streaked face. "I'm sorry, pumpkin. I'm a bad mommy, aren't I? It won't happen again, I promise."

A big, sloppy lump formed in Shane's throat as he watched woman and child together. If he were prone to fantasies, this might be one of them. To have a family like this....He gave himself a mental shake, reminding himself that he was married to his job; that he'd been there, done that, and had failed to juggle both marriage and his career. There wasn't a woman on earth who was capable of understanding his dedication.

He knew that, so there was no use fantasizing about something that could never be. A man was missing from the picture, but it was just because of the circumstances.

He wasn't that man; it was best he remember that important fact.

As Lee laid the baby on the bed to change her, Shane rushed forward to help, handing her a diaper, baby wipes, the powder, and generally getting in the way almost as much as Buck. When the baby was freshly changed, Lee picked her up again, smiling into her round little face.

"Are you hungry, sweetheart? Uncle Shane has ravioli, something I think you might like. Wanna try some?"

Her soft voice turned Shane's blood to liquid silver. He found himself almost envying Molly, and definitely admiring Lee for her efforts to play Mommy when she had no recollection of *being* one.

Then it sank in, what she'd called him. Uncle Shane. He was an only child, so he had thought he would never be an uncle, yet without hesitation, Lee had just made him one to a dark-eyed angel named Molly.

And it thrilled him to no end. *Him.* A known workaholic who got more thrills out of cleaning his gun than he did watching the Super Bowl. A man more comfortable in the company of his dog than he was with people.

"What? You want to go to Uncle Shane?"

Shane was startled and pleased to find Molly reaching for him, the inevitable drool wetting her chin. He scooped her up and lifted her high in the air, making her shriek.

"I think she's teething," Lee said, smiling as she

watched them.

A stream of drool hit Shane square in the eye. He chuckled. "I think you're right." Juggling the baby with one arm, he used his free hand to wipe his eye with the tail of his shirt.

"If—if you don't mind taking her into the kitchen, I think I'll follow your advice and change into something warmer."

Shane locked his gaze on hers, and the air instantly heated between them. He knew she was thinking about the same thing *he* was—that flaming kiss in front of the pantry. If Molly hadn't cried out, how far would it have gone?

****

Shane stared at Molly with a mixture of horror and disgust. "Maybe the ravioli was a bad idea."

His statement sent a wave of nausea pounding through Lee. She stumbled to her feet and grabbed a dish cloth, swiping ineffectively at the orange glob Molly had become. Her movements were agitated and almost fearful. "I—you're right; I shouldn't have given her the ravioli, but I think I can get her shirt clean—"

"Lee."

She stilled as Shane grabbed her hand, lifting a wounded, guilty gaze to his. "I can repaint the walls—"

"Lee," Shane said again, gently. He was frowning, searching her face as if he saw something that deeply disturbed him.

Trembling now, she gave her chin a belated tilt and looked him in the eyes. She felt an odd rush of courage rise inside her. "I'm sorry, but she's just a baby. She doesn't know what she's doing." Inwardly, she cringed, thinking about the splattered walls and the sauce-stained floor around Molly's high chair. It was hard to believe Molly had taken a single bite, considering the enormity of the mess. She didn't really blame Shane for being upset. She had once again made a gross error in judgment—

"I don't give a damn about the mess," Shane said roughly, still frowning. "And stop looking at me as if you expect me to start shouting."

"But you said it was a bad idea—"

"I didn't mean it literally, and I wasn't criticizing you."

Lee was just as confused by her surprise as Shane appeared to be. "You weren't? I mean, it's okay if you were, because it was a stupid idea to give her the—"

"It wasn't a stupid idea." His fingers closed around her hand and squeezed gently, and there was a hint of pity in his gaze. "Although it's hard to imagine from the looks of her, I think she ate a lot of the ravioli." He took the dish towel from her unresisting fingers and tossed it on the table. "I don't think this dish towel will make a dent, do you? I'll start the bath water."

"You're—you're not angry?" She braced herself, half-expecting him to change his mind and blast her with a long lecture on impulsive behavior and the consequences. And *why* was she expecting it? She didn't know him, and he'd given her no indication that he was the lecturing type.

"Of course not."

He made her feel silly for even *thinking* he might be angry. She rubbed a sudden ache at her temples, feeling impossibly confused. What did it all mean?

"Glee!" Molly screeched.

Lee turned to her just in time to catch a half-eaten ravioli square in the neck. It slid slowly down, coming to a halt at the opening of her soft cotton shirt. "I think," Lee told Molly as she calmly plucked the food from her cleavage. "That next time *I'll* do the feeding."

Molly grinned, burying both hands in her sticky hair as if she was auditioning for an herbal shampoo commercial. "Uck! Glee!" She strained to peer over her tray at Buck, who was kind enough to clean up the floor. "Uck!" The dog obediently looked up at her, his tongue lolling to the side as if he was smiling, before he resumed his job.

With grim determination, Lee began undressing the food-coated munchkin. By the time she was finished, she and Molly definitely looked related. "We look like orange popsicles," Lee told her as she hoisted the baby from the chair and headed for the bathroom.

Out of the kindness of her heart, Molly clinched the likeness by burying one of her sauce-coated hands in Lee's hair. Lee groaned, but couldn't resist a wry chuckle. "You are so gracious, Molly. Now we *really* resemble orange popsicles."

"I don't know," Shane said, emerging from the tiny bathroom and wisely plastering himself against the wall to let them pass. "You kind of remind me of the ravioli twins."

Lee stuck out her tongue at him. "Very funny, Mr. Clean. There's no such thing." She was tempted to veer closer so Molly could spread the love. It would serve him right for making fun of them.

Depositing an orange, naked Molly into the tub, Lee got her first lesson in bathing a one-year-old who preferred to spend her time splashing instead of washing. As she chased Molly around the tub with a soapy cloth, she was very conscious of Shane standing in the doorway. Every so often, she heard him chuckle or smother a laugh.

She wanted to be mad, but found herself smiling instead. "Just one more rinse, Molly, and we'll be done, okay?"

But Molly wasn't listening. Clutching the rim, she walked constantly around the tub, stopping now and then to swipe at the water and shower Lee with it. Each time she managed to hit her mark, she let out a shriek of pure glee, giving Lee the impression she'd done the very same thing many times before.

Soaked, itchy, and growing weary, Lee perched on the edge of the tub and leaned over to make one more swipe through Molly's hair.

Molly turned suddenly, grabbed Lee's arm, and began to slide under it. Lee reacted instinctively, reaching for the baby with both arms.

In the process, she lost her balance.

The splash she made rendered Molly momentarily breathless, since a wave of water hit the baby square in the face. Molly sucked in a sharp breath, blinking water drops from her eyelashes. Her tiny mouth puckered.

Lee, nearly immersed in the water, began to laugh helplessly at Molly's shocked expression.

It was enough to reassure Molly, whose mouth changed from an ominous pucker to a lop-sided grin. She clapped her hands. "Glee! Glee!"

Shane's shadow loomed over them. Lee looked up into his amused face, suddenly aware that her wet shirt was plastered to her chest. His quick, hot gaze told her that he was also aware.

"I'll take it from here." Towel in hand, he reached for the slippery Molly and lifted her from the tub. She squealed and peddled her feet, spraying Lee with more water. As if she wasn't already half-drowned.

"I—I'll just finish my bath," she said a little breathlessly, wondering if there was anything more appealing to a woman than the sight of a handsome man holding a beautiful baby. It certainly got *her* blood pumping!

The moment the door closed, she pulled the stopper and scrambled from the tub. At the rate she and Molly were going, she mused as she peeled off her wet jeans and shirt, they would be out of clothes before long.

Did Shane take his laundry all the way into Asheville when he needed clean clothes? she wondered. She plugged the stopper into the hole and turned on the water, trying to imagine a rugged man like Shane doing laundry. The image made her smile. He wasn't married, so of course he had to do his own laundry, unless he used a laundering service.

She paused in the process of soaping her hair as a disturbing possibility occurred to her. What if he *was* married? He hadn't said, and she hadn't asked. He wasn't wearing a ring, but Lee knew that didn't necessarily mean there wasn't a wife waiting from him in Asheville.

And why did the possibility disturb her? How could she feel possessive of someone she'd just met? She closed her eyes and sighed, deciding her confusion must be a result of her amnesia. Shane might be a stranger, but he wasn't any stranger than anyone else in her world at the moment. In fact, she knew more about *him* than she did her own husband.

If there was a husband.

Back to the old distressed damsel/shining knight syndrome, she thought, leaning back to rinse her hair. She felt close to Shane because he had saved her life. Nothing more, nothing less.

Okay, so there was a definite attraction between them, a magnetic pull that seemed to go into effect the moment they both entered the same room. How could she be certain she wasn't just reacting to him that way because he'd rescued her? She blew out a frustrated sigh and soaped her legs, wishing she'd thought to grab a disposable razor from her suitcase. A wry laugh escaped her. What was she thinking? She hadn't planned on bathing in the middle of the day! Molly had left her with no choice.

Molly. Lee's breath caught on a small moan. How could she not remember sweet, smiling Molly? She glanced down at her flat stomach, willing herself to remember it rounded with pregnancy.

The only thing she got for her efforts was a sharp pain behind the eyes.

****

Shane was standing in front of the fire when Lee emerged from the bathroom. He had arranged the furniture around Molly, creating a safe environment for the rambunctious baby to zip around in her walker.

Buck had discovered he could leap onto the couch to avoid getting rammed by the walker. As Lee watched, the dog bounded onto the couch, barked as if to taunt the squealing baby, then bounded down again. The moment Buck hit the floor, Molly raced after him. For a comical moment, Buck scrambled for traction on the slick floor. In the nick of time, he escaped Molly's determined efforts to pin him into a corner.

"I never knew Buck liked children," Shane said.

His comment drew her gaze to his broad shoulders. He'd pushed the sleeves of his burgundy sweatshirt to his elbows, and there was a sprinkling of white powder across his chest. Baby powder, Lee realized, her lips twitching.

With great effort, she fought a smile as she said, "How long have you had him?"

"Six years. Found him at the bottom of a ravine in a gunny sack. There were five puppies in the sack. He was the only one still alive. The rest had starved."

She swallowed a sudden lump, not bothering to hide her contempt. "How can anyone be so cruel?"

Shane's dark eyes bored into hers. "I've seen worse."

70

Lee knew he had. She could tell by the hard glint in his eyes, and in the way his jaw visibly tightened. She had a feeling Shane Knox had seen things that would give *her* nightmares. The thought evoked an instant, sincere respect for this man and his profession. To do what Shane did, day in and day out, had to require a great strength and unrelenting patience.

Had she always admired law enforcement? Did this indicate she was a good citizen? She gnawed her lip in frustration, nearly jumping when Shane spoke.

"Come on in and have a seat. I won't bite."

His mocking drawl made her flush. She hadn't realized she'd been standing in the doorway. Taking a seat on the sofa, she pulled her legs beneath her and tried to relax. It wasn't easy, with Shane looking at her with an intensity that made her want to squirm.

She concentrated on the splash of baby powder on his shirt. How scary could a man be, covered in baby powder?

"Who are you running from, Lee?"

Her eyes went wide at his abrupt question. She frowned, shaking her head. "I don't know. You *know* that I don't know."

His voice remained soft, yet relentless. "You were frightened of me earlier, when I made the comment about Molly making a mess."

"I'm not frightened of anyone," she said, thrusting out her chin.

"You thought I was going to yell at you."

"I did not."

"You did." Shane moved toward her, making her tense. "You thought I was going to ridicule you and yell at you for letting Molly get happy with the ravioli."

She looked up at him, her eyes burning. "If you're trying to make me remember something, it's not working. I don't know why I acted the way I did, but I'm not a coward!"

"I never said you were a coward."

"You implied it."

"Someone has yelled at you in the past."

"I'm sure my parents did a time or two. Didn't yours?" Her face was burning, along with her eyes. She wished he'd move away and stop nagging her. The memory of her earlier reaction embarrassed her, as if she'd been caught doing something wrong.

"Maybe it wasn't your parents. Maybe it was your husband."

"So what if it was?" she asked flippantly. "Couples argue. Or don't you know that? Have you ever been married, Shane?" Her bold as brass question surprised him, she saw. But he was obviously on to her attempt to change the subject. Why must the subject always be about *her?* she wondered peevishly.

"Yes. Once. A long time ago."

He clipped out each word as if he'd carved them from ice, warning her to drop her line of questioning. *"You've got to be ruthless. Don't give up. Keep the questions coming until you get to the truth."*

The voice again, a voice she didn't recognize, but felt compelled to obey. She shook her head, ignoring Shane's warning. "And did you and your wife ever fight?"

"Yes."

If ever a word had been uttered through clenched teeth, this was it. Lee eyed the tight set of his mouth and the blackness of his eyes. "And did you ever yell at her?"

He hesitated, his eyes narrowing. "I don't remember."

"Well," Lee said triumphantly, "I don't remember, either. What you saw earlier was—was—" She waved a dismissing hand in the air. "Just my embarrassment over ruining your floor and the walls."

"You weren't embarrassed. You were upset and anxious that *I* would be upset."

Lee let out an exasperated sigh. "You're making a mountain out of a molehill, Shane."

"Am I?"

"Yes, you are! Why don't you stick to the facts? You've obviously got one heck of an imagination."

"Do I?"

"Stop asking me questions!" she shouted suddenly and surprisingly, clutching her head.

Buck skidded to a halt and whined, his tail thumping on the floor. Molly stopped her mad racing to look anxiously at Lee.

As for Shane's expression, Lee couldn't say. She glowered at him, blaming him for making her lose her temper. "Next time you decide to play shrink, would you mind waiting until Molly's asleep?"

"I'm sorry. You're right, of course." He reached out and touched her cheek, frowning. "You're crying. I didn't mean to make you cry."

Bemused at the sudden change in him, Lee sniffled and eyed him warily. One moment he was relentless, the next he was repentant. Which was the real Shane Knox? And he thought *she* was a basket case!

"Are you still angry with me?" he asked softly, huskily. "I'm only trying to help you, you know."

Lee rubbed her eyes, then stared at his shirt. "How can I stay angry at a man who smells like baby powder?" Just as quickly as she'd frowned, she laughed at his disgruntled expression.

Shane reached down and pulled her to her feet, drawing her against him until they were nearly nose to nose. His eyes glinted with a reckless fire that knocked the air from her lungs. He touched her nose with his fingertip. "I'm glad you uncovered your freckles."

A warm gush of pleasure flooded her belly. She licked her lips, trying to decide if she believed him. "What—what kind of man *likes* freckles?" she whispered, so very aware of every single inch where they touched.

Behind them, Molly and Buck had resumed their endless game.

Shane tipped her chin, his breath warm on her face, his voice low and husky. "The kind of man who also likes huge violet eyes, silky hair, and a laugh that should be outlawed."

Mesmerized by his liquid gaze, Lee said, "You—you don't know me."

"Maybe that's the attraction."

She jerked back as if he'd slapped her. She didn't understand her reaction, but neither could she ignore it or the pain his careless comment caused. He liked her because he didn't know her.

Which meant...if he knew her, he might *not* like her. Suddenly, Lee felt very certain she was right. Shane Knox wouldn't like the real Lee Whoever-she-was.

"What is it?" he demanded.

Lee stepped away and shook her head, unwilling to give him an honest answer. He wouldn't understand.

Chapter Seven

After three days of blizzard-like conditions, the storm had taken a break.

"Are you positive you won't come with me?" Shane asked the next morning, glancing worriedly at Lee. She stood at the window looking out into the winter wonderland, her jaw thrust out in a now-familiar way.

Although it had stopped snowing, the temperature was still well below freezing. Shane could only hope the snow plows had done their job and the interstate was open. They not only needed baby formula and diapers, but he needed fuel for the generator.

He folded the list he'd made and slid it into his pocket. On the back of the list was information on Lee and Molly's whereabouts, should something happen to him during his trip to Asheville. He would have felt better if she had agreed to go with him, but she had refused.

"I told you, I don't want to go," she said without turning around.

She might not have noticed that panicky note in her voice, but Shane did. He bit his tongue to keep from pushing her. She had let him know loud and clear yesterday that she wouldn't be pushed.

"Don't forget," he began, only to be drowned out by her exasperated sigh.

"I know, I know. If you don't come back, sit tight and someone will come eventually." She turned to look at him, her gaze skimming over him in a way that warmed him more than any fire could. "If I have to, I'm to use the powdered milk in the pantry for Molly. The wood pile is against the left side of the cabin, and if the generator stalls, I'm to prime it three times before I restart it."

Her sudden vulnerable look made his heart do a triple somersault, and reminded him it was definitely time to end his little fantasy.

Because that's what Lee and Molly were becoming, he acknowledged, avoiding her gaze as he shrugged into his thick coat and pulled on his gloves. Disgusted with himself, he spoke more harshly than he intended, "Don't go outside unless you absolutely have to. There are bears and wolves around these parts, not to mention—"

"Hungry mountain lions," she supplied with studied patience. Then she spoiled it by adding, "But you're coming back, aren't you, Shane? Nothing is going to happen to you."

His gaze met hers. Sparks leaped and crackled between them. "Nothing is going to happen to me," he assured her.

He went to the open doorway of the bedroom to take one last look at the sleeping baby, satisfied with their combined efforts to keep her safe. They had pushed the bed against the wall, then cushioned the floor around the bed with pillows and blankets. If Molly *did* take a tumble from the bed, he didn't think it would hurt anything more than her pride.

Returning to the living room, he approached Lee, who stood hugging herself and looking lost, yet at the same time determined. He felt that familiar kick in his gut again, followed by a dangerous yearning. *She belongs to someone else,* he reminded himself.

The reminder didn't stop him from reaching out and cupping her jaw with his gloved hand. He leaned forward slowly, giving her time to protest. When she didn't, he closed the distance between his mouth and hers.

Her lips were soft and responsive, and the little sigh he heard stirred his imagination.

As if it *needed* stirring.

He pulled away, his warm gaze searching her face, remembering each freckle, recalling every scorching kiss. They had known each other three days, yet Shane felt as if he were leaving a part of himself behind.

Dangerous, impossible feelings.

All the more reason to get away from her, to start the search for her identity. Molly and Lee weren't his to keep. "I'll see you tonight."

"Okay. Be careful."

A bitter wind caught him the moment he stepped outside, reminding him that although the snow had stopped, it wasn't that far gone. To emphasize the warning, it took several moments before Shane could get the driver's side door open; the doors were frozen shut.

The four-wheel drive jeep started after a second's hesitation. Shane let the engine warm, his thoughts on the journey ahead and the woman and child he was leaving behind. He hadn't told Lee he planned to drop by the police station and find out if there had been any inquiries about her.

After the way she'd panicked when he suggested she and Molly go with him, he had decided to keep the information to himself. If he found out anything, he would have to tell her, of course.

If he didn't...well, then, she wouldn't have worried needlessly. *Why* she worried about such a discovery remained a mystery.

Shane flipped on the heater. Warm air rushed from the stale vents, chasing the chill from his bones. After a few moments, he was able to remove his gloves. The tires whined as they plowed through the heavy snowdrifts covering the narrow lane.

Shane kept both hands on the wheel, forcing himself to concentrate until he reached the interstate.

It was slow going, and often Shane was forced to shift into low gear to get through a particularly deep bank of snow. The road itself was completely obliterated and it was purely by instinct and memory that Shane was able to navigate it. An unsuspecting traveler would have no such luck.

It took him an hour to travel the three miles from his cabin to the interstate, which, thankfully, was reasonably clear. As he carefully merged with the traffic, Shane let his thoughts drift back to Lee.

Why had she looked so devastated when he'd teasingly suggested her attraction was due to the fact that he didn't know her? Had someone in her past undermined her self-esteem, her self-confidence? Shane's teeth clicked together as he considered the possibility. Lee was graceful, beautiful, and obviously a loving, caring person, if her interaction with Molly was any indication. What manner of person had been blind to the obvious?

It was only fair, he mused, that he examine the few flaws he'd discovered about Lee. Like the way she had badgered him about his ex-wife. Her rapid-fire questions had reminded him of Bobby Dillon's sleazy defense lawyer. The man had questioned him right into a corner, leaving him no time to realize where the questions were heading.

"Did you or did you not hit my client, Officer Knox?"

Shane had responded honestly. *"Yes, but—"*

"But what, Officer Knox? Are you saying just because my client hit his wife, that makes him a murderer? Wouldn't that be a pot calling the kettle black?"

"No—"

"Let's stick to the facts. You just admitted you hit my client. Does that make you a possible murder

suspect?"

Shane gave his head a quick shake, forcing his fingers to relax where they held the steering wheel in a death grip. That damned lawyer had twisted everything around until it looked as if Shane was the suspect, not Bobby Dillon.

Lee had said, *"Let's stick to the facts."* That didn't necessarily mean she was a lawyer, Shane argued with the logical side of his brain. It was just as possible that she was married to a lawyer. In fact, her father or brother could be a lawyer.

Since he didn't want to think about a husband, Shane tried to zero in on the father and brother possibilities and pushed the husband possibility aside. But he knew it was madness to ignore the obvious. Hell, she wore a wedding band! Yet he couldn't bring himself to believe she was well and truly married.

She didn't kiss like a married woman.

But then, he reminded himself ruthlessly, she didn't remember being married.

Then there were the disturbing similarities to his obsessive ex-wife, Darla. The way Lee had arranged his pantry so the can goods were in alphabetical order. He'd come home from pulling a double-shift to find his ex-wife doing the very same thing.

Only her excuse had been a blistering accusation. She was bored, because he was never home. He was married to his job, so why did he need her?

As it turned out, he *hadn't* needed her, and she was now happily married to someone else. Someone who came home at the same time every day, and didn't work on weekends or holidays. Shane didn't have what it took to make a good marriage, and he knew it.

He recalled Lee's embarrassed flush when he'd

asked her what she was doing, arranging his canned goods. His lips curved, not in contempt, but in surprised amusement. Her expression had reminded him of the many times his mother had caught him stealing cookies from the pan before they had a chance to cool.

An endearing, guilty look that was a far cry from his ex-wife's bitter expression. Shane grimaced, knowing he was to blame for his failed marriage. He'd known his job would come first, that it would take its toll, but he hadn't listened to his instincts.

Instead, he had listened to Darla's reassurances that their love would conquer all. Shane laughed shortly. Her tune had changed quickly after the vows were said, and Shane realized that Darla had believed she could change him.

She had been wrong.

****

Lee stared at the watch she'd found in the pocket of her suitcase. It was fancy, the band made of gold, the watch-face surrounded by an impressive cluster of diamonds that looked disturbingly real. She even recognized the brand name.

The watch didn't make sense when compared to her wardrobe of cotton shirts and blue jeans. Was the fact that it out-dressed even the dressiest outfit she presumably owned the reason it was in her suitcase and not on her wrist?

Lee sensed that it was.

She looked at the time again. Two hours had passed since she had stood at the window and watched Shane back carefully down the steep incline to the lane below. Had he reached Asheville, or was he still cautiously plowing through snow on the interstate?

Thankfully, Molly had awakened shortly after Shane left, keeping her occupied. She had fed the baby a bowl of oats, which Molly seemed to prefer over scrambled eggs. Molly was now playing on the floor with a tin cup Lee had found in one of the cabinets above the sink.

The banging of the tin cup on the hardwood floor wasn't quite loud enough to cover the sound of Buck's barking. The louder Molly banged, the louder Buck barked.

Lee smiled, amazed to find the noise didn't bother her. Was this a sign? she wondered. Because she had to be either a saint or a mother to put up with the racket Molly and Buck were making.

It took her a moment to realize that Buck had stopped barking, and was now scratching anxiously at the door. Lee quickly went to the door. "You need to go potty, Buck?"

Buck barked once and wagged his tail. He looked back at Molly and barked several times, giving Lee the uncanny impression he was trying to explain to her that he would be back.

Feeling foolish, Lee unlocked the door and held it open. Buck darted through, then came to a sudden halt just outside the door.

His hackles rose. He began to growl in a menacing way that caused *Lee's* hackles to rise and sent a shiver down her spine. Slowly, she edged the door open another few inches and peered outside.

A man stood in the deep snow a few yards from the cabin door, his cautious gaze on the growling dog. He wore a heavy, fur-lined coat, boots, and gloves, yet his cheeks and nose were red from the cold.

"Easy, Buck," she said, warily eying first the bearded man, then the rifle slung over his shoulder. She remembered that Shane had said it wasn't yet hunting season. "Can I help you?"

Buck continued to growl low in his throat, a warning to the man to stay exactly where he was.

Lee didn't think he'd be moving anytime soon,

not as long as Buck felt threatened. Glancing at Molly to assure herself the baby was safely corralled, Lee eased through the door opening and pulled it closed behind her. She didn't want the baby to catch a cold by leaving the door open.

With his eye on Buck, the man said, "I was just scouting the area." He jerked his chin toward the North. "Live up the mountain a ways. Last night, a pack of wolves killed six of my chickens and mangled one of my huntin' dogs. Had to put him down."

She didn't have a clue where she was from, but Lee didn't think it was the mountains because she couldn't imagine seeing *one* live wolf, much less a pack. "Are—are you certain they were wolves?" Just the thought made Lee want to snag Buck by his collar, pull him inside, and firmly bolt the door.

The man bared his teeth in a brief smile. "You're not from around here, are you?"

For some reason, his smile irritated her. "No, I'm not." Hopefully he wouldn't ask *where* she—

"Where are you from?"

She couldn't say, *"I don't know."* Not to a stranger. So she lied. Big time. "My husband and I are—we just come here to get away once in a while." Maybe he'd believe her reddened cheeks were due to the sharp, bitterly cold wind instead of the lie she'd just told. She'd been standing outside less than five minutes, and already her fingers were numb.

"Your husband? He got a name?"

"Shane—Shane Knox." Just for good measure, she added, "He's in law enforcement."

"Is that right?" The man spit a stream of tobacco into the snow, and Buck took a menacing step in his direction.

"Buck. Stay," Lee ordered calmly.

"Is he around? Maybe I could talk to him about that pack of wolves. See if he's seen 'em around."

"I—I think he would have said something to me

if he'd seen them, Mr.—?"

"Well," he said, ignoring her question. "I'll be on my way, then. You might want to tell Mr. Knox to keep his eye out for those wolves. Hate for something to happen to his dog—" His gaze drifted from Buck to Lee. "Or his pretty little wife."

Pretty little wife? Did people actually say things like that? Lee shivered, glad when the man turned and tromped back down the hill.

She was frozen, but she waited until the man was out of sight before she grabbed Buck's collar and pulled him inside. If he needed to go that badly, she'd prefer he use the floor rather than face a pack of hungry wolves. She was already attached to the mutt, and Molly was downright in love with him. Shane, she suspected, would be bereft without his canine companion.

Buck whined and scratched at the door. Lee felt a pang of guilt as she hunkered down to eye level with the dog. "Sorry, Buck. Do you think you could wait until your master gets home? I don't want the wolves to make a meal out of you." She hesitated, then scratched his ears. "If you have to go, then just go on the floor. It can't be any worse than cleaning up after Molly."

The dog whined and wagged his tail. He cast a longing look at the door, then bounded off to play with Molly. Apparently, Lee mused, he was too well-trained to go in the house.

She hoped Shane returned soon.

****

When Shane entered the precinct, he felt as if he'd been gone for months instead of a week. He plowed his way through handshakes and back claps until he reached his partner's little slice of hell, as Kyle Grayfeather was fond of calling it.

Kyle Grayfeather was a big man in height *and* proportions. In proud keeping with his Indian heritage, he wore his long hair in two braids; each braid was liberally streaked with premature gray, adding to Kyle's proud, noble appearance.

Aside from his braids, Kyle wore his uniform like any other officer, spoke English better than most, and liked his beer cold and straight from the tap. When he spotted Shane coming his way, he rose with a grin, his black eyes twinkling. "It's about damned time you came out of hiding."

"I wasn't hiding," Shane growled good-naturedly, slapping Kyle's upraised hand. Without preamble, he came straight to the point. "Can you check lost and found for me and see if anyone's called asking about a woman and her baby—a girl around twelve months old?"

Kyle's brow rose at Shane's mysterious request. "And that's all you're going to give me?" He faked a wounded look. "Is that how you treat a partner, pardner?"

Shane hesitated. He looked around, relieved to find his co-workers now occupied with their work. Stepping closer, he lowered his voice and gave Kyle a sketchy outline of what had happened. He would have gladly performed the search, but he was on suspension, and didn't want to draw attention to himself.

By the time he finished, Kyle's brow had disappeared into his hairline. "You're saying this woman and her baby have been staying with *you?*"

His disbelieving tone amused Shane. "Down, Fido. Didn't you hear what I said? She has amnesia, a baby, *and* she's wearing a wedding band." He didn't add that those facts hadn't stopped him from kissing her.

Four times.

"I'll get right on it, Hoss. In the meantime, why don't you grab us some lunch?"

Shane decided he could use a bite himself. "Any

preferences?"

Without hesitation, Kyle said, "Two foot-long meatball subs with onions and green peppers." When Shane nodded and turned away, Kyle grabbed his arm, the humor suddenly gone from his voice. "You should probably know that Dillon's been blowing a lot of hot air around about getting you thrown off the force. Claims you ruined his reputation."

Shane's laugh came out more of a snarl. "The only reputation he has is that of a wife-beater and a murderer."

"The jury found him innocent," Kyle reminded him, his brow furrowed with worry.

"He killed her. You and I both know he killed her, Kyle." Shane suddenly lost his appetite. "If it hadn't been for his damned lawyer, he'd be where he belongs right now—waiting for his execution on death row."

"Just watch your back, my friend. The man's not stable."

Shane gave his partner a hard look, his hands clenching. "That makes two of us. If Dillon wants another round with me, he might get more than he bargained for."

Chapter Eight

It was warmer by the fire.

The temperature had dropped into the single digits, and a light snow had begun to fall. Lee, Shane, Molly and Buck gathered around the fireplace to share a delicious meal of salmon patties, tater tots, and linguini with alfredo sauce.

Molly, ensconced in her walker, definitely favored the linguini.

A long noodle hung from her hair to her shoulder. More clung to her chest and stomach, but Lee would have sworn she'd seen the baby eat every single one.

She stared at the baby in open fascination. "How does she do that? It's like her food multiplies."

"Yeah," Shane agreed, equally fascinated. "Even with Buck waiting with his mouth open, Molly manages to decorate herself with the stuff." He gave his head a baffled shake, his gaze meeting Lee's.

Lee felt liquid heat surge into her blood stream. Orange flames seemed to dance in his dark eyes. She couldn't pull her gaze away, unable to forget just how happy she'd been to see him pull into the lean-to. With extreme will power, she focused on her plate. "You shouldn't have gone to so much trouble. Molly and I were perfectly happy with chicken noodle soup and ravioli."

Shane chuckled, and the sound vibrated right down to her toasty toes.

"If you had seen the look on Margaret's face—"

"Margaret?"

"The cashier at Food Giant," he explained,

leaning forward to further upset her equilibrium by wiping at her chin with his napkin. He reached his hand in Molly's direction, then let it drop with a sigh. "Margaret's accustomed to my usual case or two of chicken noodle soup and ravioli."

Lee felt a grin tugging at her mouth at the image. "She was surprised, was she?"

Shane grinned right back at her. "I thought she would burst a seam before she finished ringing up the groceries." He gaze went to Molly, who was standing very still as Buck lapped a linguini noodle from her hand. "Just about the time I reached the door, she busted loose."

When he paused, Lee prompted, "Well? What did she say?"

"She asked me if I was OK." He shrugged, looking boyishly embarrassed. "When I told her I was fine, she asked me if I was having unexpected company up at the cabin."

Lee blinked. "She knew you were here?"

"Everyone knows I'm here, Lee. And why. Asheville isn't that big of a town."

"And you're popular guy," she said, then bit her lip. She really, really needed to start thinking before she spoke, she chided herself. "I mean, you're single and—and—"

"And?"

Her eyes narrowed with suspicion. Was he fishing for compliments? "Reasonably handsome," she said slowly, watching his face for signs of amusement. Sometimes it wasn't obvious he was teasing. This was one of those times. "Not to mention the fact that you make the best salmon cakes I've ever tasted."

The flame in his eyes settled into a slow burn. He reached out and wiped her chin again, but Lee suspected the action was useless. Whatever was there hadn't come off the first time he'd tried. *Like daughter, like mother,* she thought, glancing at Molly, who was grinning like a fool in love as Buck licked her chubby little fingers.

"How would *you* know?" he teased.

This time, Lee didn't take offense. She blushed and twirled her fork around a few noodles. "You're right; I don't know." She set her fork down on her plate, then set it aside on the floor for Buck to clean. Deliberately, she looked at him. From the moment he'd walked in the door, his arms full of grocery sacks, she'd wanted to ask the question.

She couldn't wait any longer. "Is anyone looking for us?"

He chuckled wryly. "I think we can assume your I.Q. is in the three digit zone." He set his own plate aside, casting Buck a warning glance as the dog started forward. "As for your question, no. Nobody seems to be looking for you and Molly."

Her sigh of relief was barely audible, but Lee knew from his sharp look that he'd heard. "I can't help it, Shane. I wish I could explain—"

He reached out and placed a finger to her lips. "Hey," he said softly, gently. "Why don't we just leave it alone for a while?" Rising, he held out his hands. "Let's go wash the dishes."

Lee took his hands and let him pull her to her feet. She glanced at the baby. "What about Molly?"

Instead of answering, Shane lifted Molly, walker and all, up into the air. He set her safely down inside the safe zone he'd created with the furniture, smiling at her delighted giggles at being temporarily airborne. "I think she'll be alright here, with Buck babysitting."

On cue, Buck leaped over the back of the sofa and into the blocked-off area. Molly zeroed in on him, then began to peddle her little legs in a frenzy of activity.

After watching them a moment, Lee gathered

their plates and followed Shane into the kitchen. He ran the dishwater as she started to scrape the remains of their food into the trash can.

"Wait."

Startled by his sharp command, Lee straightened from her chore with a frown.

"There are a lot of hungry critters outside," he explained, nodding toward the back door of the cabin. "With this freak blizzard, I'm sure they'd enjoy the leftovers."

His comment reminded Lee of her earlier encounter. In her excitement and relief over Shane's safe arrival, she'd forgotten to tell him about the man searching for the wolves. "Won't that attract the wolves?" she asked. "This man came by today—"

"What?" Shane barked.

Lee nearly dropped the plates. Her face suffused with heat, and she felt a strange urge to backtrack and forget about telling him. She fought the urge and ventured forth. "He—he said a pack of wolves attacked his chickens and killed one of his hunting dogs."

Shane grabbed the plates from her and dropped them into the sink. Lee was certain she heard one break.

"Why didn't you tell me about this earlier?" he demanded harshly, taking her by the shoulders.

Dismay shot through Lee. She had that strange feeling she'd done something terribly wrong, but she didn't know *what* that something was. "I—I—" She licked her lips, trying not to cower in the face of his sudden scowl. Cowering was not an option. She didn't know *why* this was important, she just knew it was. "I didn't think it was that important," she blurted out, growing stiff beneath his grip.

"Tell me everything he said."

His grip didn't lighten, and the harshness of his voice didn't relent. Lee told him everything she could remember the man saying, adding that Buck had seemed upset. There was something in Shane's eyes that frightened her, yet aroused her curiosity. It was a painful reminder that she knew virtually nothing about this man.

He said he was a cop.

She couldn't prove otherwise.

In fact, she—and Molly too—were literally at his mercy.

Oddly enough, the knowledge didn't terrify her as she suspected it should have.

"I'm not going to hurt you, Lee, so stop looking at me as if you're expecting me to."

"Maybe," she said with surprising calmness, "I wouldn't feel this way if you weren't squeezing the life out of me."

He immediately eased his hold, but didn't let her go. "The dishes can wait. I think there are a few things you need to know—for safety's sake." He released his hold long enough to snatch up her wrist. "Let's go into the living room. This might take a while."

Curiosity warred with trepidation as Lee obediently followed him.

****

Where to start? Shane brushed a hand through his hair, grimacing as he encountered a stiff linguini noodle tangled within the strands. He pulled it free and stared at it in bemusement, wondering when Molly had launched it at him, and if Lee had known about it.

With a wry shake of his head, he pitched the noodle into the fire. It crackled and sizzled.

He turned to face Lee, who had made herself as small as possible in one corner of the sofa. He'd frightened her, he realized with a pang of remorse, and she was trying very hard not to show it.

"Damn," he said very softly, but distinctly. She

paled even further, and he immediately cursed again—this time silently. "I'm not angry with you, Lee."

Her chin came out a good inch or two. "I haven't done anything wrong for you to be angry about."

"You're right, you haven't." He glanced at Molly, then did a double-take.

The baby had fallen asleep in her walker, her head tilted forward to rest on the desk surface. Before he could start her way, Lee jumped from the couch and headed for the baby.

"I'll take her to bed," she said, almost defiantly.

Shane watched her go, knowing he'd handled the situation all wrong. Well, he mused wryly, he had about five minutes to figure out how to make it right.

She was back in *less* than five.

Resuming her position on the couch—this time less defensively, Shane noted—she tilted her chin again and waited.

He cleared his throat, forced himself to look at her, then began. "The captain had his reasons for placing me on suspension. Last year, I answered a domestic violence call reported by a woman named Sandra Dillon. Her husband was beating her. By the time my partner and I got there, Bobby Dillon had knocked out three of her teeth, and busted her nose. He was drunk and high on his victory." Shane swallowed a ball of disgust at the memory. "He was like a madman, resisting arrest and swinging at anything that moved."

"He hit you?" she guessed shrewdly.

"Yes." Shane tensed the moment he uttered the word. Her voice was expressionless, although her face revealed a dawning horror as she guessed what was to come. "I had to defend myself, so I stunned him with my billy-club. His sleazy lawyer made a big stink, and Dillon walked before daylight. He went straight to Sandra and beat her to death. Literally."

Shane turned around and braced his hand on the mantel, staring into the fire and deliberately, painfully, evoking that unforgettable night. "I arrested Dillon and brought him in, but not without a fight. I think Dillon knew exactly what he was doing, taunting me the way he did. I lost control."

"And he walked," she breathed, horror evident in her hushed voice. "Oh, God."

"Yeah." Shane laughed without humor. "Somewhere along the way, I forgot that a perp could beat the hell out of a cop, but a cop couldn't defend himself, unless he wanted to get slapped with a police brutality charge. It didn't help that the lawyer discovered Sandra and I had dated back in high school. He managed to twist *that* around, as well."

"What—what about your partner? Wasn't he a witness?"

Shane shook his head. "I wouldn't let Kyle go with me to arrest him. This was between me and Dillon, and I didn't want Kyle to get involved."

"You shouldn't have gone alone."

"Yeah, well." Shane turned to pin her with his gaze. He jolted at the fire blazing from her eyes. His face softened, and his heart felt as if it was melting into a puddle at his feet. "I guess I wasn't looking at the big picture. I guess at the time I believed in justice."

"You don't anymore." It wasn't a question.

"Of course I do." But he could tell she didn't believe him. "Just not as much as I did before Dillon."

"Why are you telling me this now?"

"Because I think maybe the man you saw today was Dillon. Can you remember what he looked like?"

"He had a dark beard, but that's about the only distinguishing thing I can remember."

"Dillon wears a beard, and his hair is dark."

She blanched, and Shane felt a sharp kick in his gut. If he had Dillon before him now..."Don't worry. It's me he's after."

"I wasn't worried about me," she countered swiftly. "I'm worried about you."

"Why?"

"Because—" she stopped, swallowed hard. "Because you saved my life—"

"Still sticking to that old standby?" he teased.

Her gaze never faltered, and she didn't smile. "And because I know you're a good man, and a good cop." She made a sour face. "No wonder you hate lawyers."

"I don't hate them," Shane denied. "I just don't like them. Hate is a strong word."

"Maybe not misplaced in your situation."

"Just as there are good people and bad people, I'm sure there are good lawyers and bad lawyers. Same goes for cops."

She finally smiled. "I may have lost my memory, but I haven't lost my mind. Most cops are good." Her voice dipped to a whisper. *"You* are."

"There are people who wouldn't agree with you."

She flung her head back and shot him a challenging look, giving Shane a rare glimpse of the strong woman he suspected she was. "They didn't see what you saw, did they?"

Shane stared at her for a long moment before he said with a hint of seriousness, "Has anyone ever told you that you'd make a great lawyer?" When her eyes widened in horror, he laughed, thinking she mocked him. "No, seriously."

"Seriously! I'm not a lawyer. I'm too short—"

"Short? What does short have to do with it?"

She ignored his question. "And I'm clumsy, and I have a million freckles—"

"A *few*. You have a *few* freckles, Lee. And you are definitely not clumsy. In fact, I've never seen a more graceful woman. You move like a dancer."

She laughed in outright disbelief. "Aren't we a pair? Stroking each other's egos—"

"You were stroking my ego?" he asked in mock chagrin, making her laugh harder.

They shared a humorous moment that seemed suspended in time, before they both finally sobered. Lee once again tucked her legs beneath her on the couch. Shane fought the urge to sit beside her, throw his arms around her, and hug her tightly, as if he had the right.

He was almost relieved when she filled the sudden void.

"Tell me about your life, Shane. Maybe it will help me to remember mine."

Shane took the chair beside the sofa, stretching his legs out before him and lacing his hands across his stomach. He rested his head on the back of the chair and sighed. "There's not much to tell. I'm an only child. My father was a Federal Marshal, and was hardly ever home. Mom worked mostly, I think, to keep from being lonely when Dad was on the road hunting down escaped criminals. I had a pretty normal childhood. Played football, made decent grades." He lifted his head to look at her and found her watching him avidly.

She blushed and looked away, and Shane had to bite back a smile.

"When did you realize you wanted to be a cop?"

"When my father got killed." He heard her sharp intake of breath, and felt a rush of warmth at her compassion. "It was two weeks before my graduation from high school. He got shot in the chest, and he wasn't wearing a vest. I remember being furious with him for a long time about that. He was a Federal Marshal. He was supposed to know better."

"Who—who shot him?"

Shane didn't care if his ironic laugh was

inappropriate. "An old woman. Dad was after her grandson, who had jumped bond on a murder charge. She shot him with a shotgun at close range. His partners said he never saw it coming. She was a gray-haired little old lady who didn't look as if she'd have the strength to *lift* a shotgun, much less fire it."

"Maybe it was his time to go," Lee murmured.

"And maybe it was sheer stupidity on my dad's part for underestimating the situation."

"You mean, like you did with Dillon?"

"Ouch. You don't pull any punches, do you?"

"Should I?"

He felt her warm fingers curl around his forearm, sending a streak of white-hot lightning straight into his heart. Her touch alone could send his pulse sky-rocketing. What would it be like to make love with her? Would he survive the experience? At that moment, Shane discovered he wanted to find out.

Wanted it very, very badly.

"Shane...you've got to stop blaming yourself for Sandra's death. *You* didn't kill her. Her husband did."

"If I hadn't—"

"Then he would have waited until another day," she inserted in a rough, husky voice that betrayed her sympathy. "From what you've told me, it was just a matter of time. Short of killing *him,* you probably couldn't have stopped him."

"Then maybe I should have." Shane clenched his teeth as the image of Sandra Dillon's beaten body came to mind. When they'd found her, her eyes had been open and staring.

That image haunted his dreams.

The soft, warm fingers on his arm disappeared. Shane sucked in a bereft breath, only to hold it in his lungs when Lee settled her small frame onto his lap.

He kept his eyes closed, stunned by her action. Had she read his mind?

One arm curled around his neck. Her fingers delved into his hair at the nape and began to absently filter through the layers.

Shane finally dared to open his eyes and look at her, so very conscious of her soft bottom pressing into his hardness. Did she feel it? Would it frighten her?

Her huge eyes were luminous in the firelight. Somberly, she said, "If you had killed Bobby Dillon to keep him from killing his wife, then you would have gone to prison. If you had gone to prison, you wouldn't have been *here*, and Molly and I most likely would have died." She leaned forward, staring at his mouth with a very clear want shining in her eyes.

And he was just a man, wasn't he? A lonely man who had finally found the woman of his dreams, only to realize she belonged to another.

The reminder stilled his forward movement, but it didn't stop him from accepting her kiss. How could he think of rejecting *this?*

Chapter Nine

She didn't want to think about *why* she was kissing a man she hardly knew. She didn't want to consider the consequences later, should she find out she had a husband she loved.

Right then, as she lay in Shane's arms, all that was certain in Lee's life was the fact that she *wanted* to be here. She *wanted* to kiss him, and she wanted him to kiss her back.

From the moment their mouths touched, Lee tasted the hunger on his lips, and an answering hunger flared inside of her. She moaned and pressed closer, winding her arms around his neck. She opened her mouth to allow him to deepen the kiss, and he obeyed.

The kiss wasn't their first, yet it held all the excitement and passion of the first. Their tongues melded, dueled, then retreated. She couldn't get close enough to satisfy the ache his kisses created.

As if he sensed her need—*as if he knew her*—he shifted her until she lay on top of him. He caught her breathless moan in his throat, his big hands sliding down to cup her bottom and press her tightly against him.

It was Buck's low, warning growl that intruded on their passion.

Lee found herself back on the sofa in one, swift move. Dazed, she stared at Shane, who was standing now and watching Buck at the door. Shane's hair stood on end in the back where she'd ruffled it, and his chest rose and fell rapidly.

It was the only outward sign that he'd gotten as

lost as she had in the kiss.

"What is it?" she whispered, looking at Buck.

"Someone's out there." Shane's narrowed gaze snapped to her, then back to Buck. He strode to the door, grabbed his coat and gun. "Lock the door after me."

Panic shot Lee from the couch to the door in seconds. She grabbed his arm, forgetting he was a trained police officer. Forgetting he wasn't hers to panic over. Forgetting she shouldn't care so much about a man she barely knew. "Don't go! Don't go out there, Shane, please!"

He placed a reassuring hand over hers, his eyes black as night and just as mysterious. "Nothing's going to happen to me, Lee. I promise."

"But --" Her mouth went dry. She swallowed hard. "What if it does? What if Dillon's out there, just waiting for you to open that door so he can take a shot at you?" Her burgeoning terror made her reckless. She tried to shake his rock-hard arm, but couldn't budge it. "What if you're about to make the same mistake your dad made with the grandmother?"

She saw him waver, and knew instinctively that he wasn't thinking about his own safety, but of her and Molly. Shamelessly, she took advantage of the knowledge. "If you open that door, the light will be behind you. Dillon could be out there in the woods with his rifle pointed right at you. You'd be dead before you ever stepped outside. Where would that leave me and Molly, Shane? Will you at least wait until daylight, when you'll have the same advantage as Dillon?"

"You present a damned good case, Counselor."

For once, she ignored his insinuation that she might be the very thing he detested. "Please, Shane? Wait until morning?"

His jaw clenched. He stared at her for a long

moment. Finally, he sighed and returned his coat to the hook, shoving his gun back into the holster. "Until morning," he agreed, albeit begrudgingly. "Go to bed, Lee, before I forget there's a ring on your finger."

Lee opened her mouth to tell him that she didn't care, but in the end she knew he was right. Maybe she didn't remember a husband, and maybe she didn't care right now, but Shane hadn't lost his memory. He had the decency to cool their passion before she did something she might later regret.

Another reason to admire him. Was there no end to the good things she was discovering about Shane?

****

She went to bed, but she didn't fall asleep until hours later. As a result, she was groggy and disoriented when Shane shook her awake at dawn.

"Lee," he whispered close to her ear. "Get up and lock the door behind me."

His statement brought her fully awake. She glanced at the window, saw that it was daylight, and closed her eyes.

She should have known Shane wouldn't change his mind about going out.

Untangling Molly's fist from her hair, Lee slipped quietly out of bed and followed Shane to the door. The floor was frigid on her bare feet. Buck, who was crouched at her side, didn't seem to mind the cold. He wagged a hopeful tail at Shane, but for once, Shane ignored the dog.

He paused at the door, staring down into her upturned face. "I'm just going to take a look around, see if I can tell if he's been snooping around."

"And if you find him?" Lee folded her arms over her chest to combat the chill seeping around the door. "What then?"

"Then I'll ask him what his intentions are, and warn him to stay away from here." He reached out and tipped her chin. His voice was suddenly hoarse as he said, "You're beautiful in the morning."

Weakness flooded Lee's knees. She braced her hand against the wall to support herself. "You're trying to distract me."

"No." He smiled when she looked unconvinced. "I meant what I said, and if I didn't need to go, I would prove it to you."

Lee briefly considered using her womanly wiles to try and stop him from going, but one glance into his determined eyes told her it wouldn't work. "When will you be back?"

"As soon as I can."

What kind of answer was that? Lee sighed and pushed her hair from her eyes. "Please be careful."

"I will."

A blast of cold air mingled with ice crystals hit her as Shane opened the door. It wasn't snowing, but the day was overcast and the wind had kicked up, blowing the powdery snow around until it resembled a mini blizzard.

When he pulled the door closed behind him, Lee obediently slid the bolt home. If not for Molly, she might have insisted on going with him, she mused, heading for the kitchen to make herself a cup of instant hot chocolate. Buck followed her.

Each time she stopped, he stopped and sat on his haunches.

She opened the pantry door, smiling at the jumble of assorted canned goods, cereals, and packages piled on the shelves. Shane had gone overboard with the shopping, but she had to admit she was grateful. She plucked a package of cocoa mix from the open box and closed the door on the chaos. If she grew bored, she could always straighten things.

She paused, realizing the urge to put things in order had faded. With a shrug, she pushed the thought aside.

After a leisurely cup of cocoa in front of the fire, Lee got dressed, then tidied up the cabin. Just as she was rinsing the last dish in the kitchen, she heard Molly.

Buck barked and bounded ahead of her, jumping on the bed and licking Molly's face until she was giggling helplessly. Smiling, Lee shooed him down. "Good morning, Molly."

Molly let out a string of unintelligible garble and held out her arms. Lee picked her up, squeezing her and inhaling her sweet baby smells. Her heart kicked as Molly's arms tightened around her neck, returning the hug.

Lee's eyes stung. Was Molly her child? How could she forget such a wonderful baby? Old questions Lee couldn't stop asking herself, and was it any wonder? What type of person forgot their own child? Yes, she'd sustained a head injury, which had most probably caused her amnesia. But it had been four days now, and the injury hadn't been *that* bad. In fact, the bump was gone, leaving only a superficial scratch.

Maybe Shane was right, Lee mused, settling Molly into the high chair. She began to prepare the baby a bowl of oats as Molly banged a spoon against the plastic tray on her high chair. Maybe there *was* a more sinister reason behind her memory loss.

With a sigh, Lee pushed her dark thoughts aside and concentrated on feeding the baby. Each time she brought the spoon near Molly's mouth, Molly attempted to grab it. Lee deftly held it out of reach, swooping in when she saw an opening. Molly loved the game, squealing when she got lucky enough to grab the spoon and knock the oats onto the tray. Lee had gotten smart, however, and kept a damp hand towel on standby, swiping up the mess before Molly had a chance to smear it everywhere.

If the food managed to reach the floor, she knew Buck was ready and willing to help clean up.

After breakfast, Lee took Molly into the living room and sat on the floor with her, playing with the baby and Buck until she realized she was just a third wheel. Smiling, she left the happy twosome in the safety area and went to make the bed.

Domestic chores, she mused as she fluffed the pillows, wishing she could remember another time and place when she'd most likely performed the same chore. *Why couldn't she remember?*

The question continued to nag her as she cleaned the bathroom, checked on Molly, then went to straighten the pantry. When she wasn't thinking about her situation, she was thinking about Shane.

She glanced at the fancy watch she'd put on after Shane left, noting that he'd been gone for three hours now. Where was he? Wasn't he cold? Had he found Dillon? Had something happened?

Over the next two hours, as she imagined every possible horrible scenario, Lee's worry turned into floor-pacing anxiety. How could anyone stay out in that type of weather this long? She tried to assure herself that Shane was perfectly capable of taking care of himself, but after another hour, that assurance ceased to comfort her.

Something bad must have happened. What if Dillon had been lying in wait, and Shane was now lying in the snow somewhere, possibly bleeding to death?

And there was absolutely nothing she could do. She couldn't take Molly out in the cold, and she couldn't leave her alone.

Lee hated feeling helpless. She paced. She wrung her hands. She stoked the fire until flames roared up the chimney. Maybe, she thought, half-mad with worry, if Shane saw the smoke, he would think the cabin was on fire and come running.

If he could.

She cursed the fact that the cabin had no phone. She cursed the fact that *she* had no phone. Who traveled without a cell phone these days? she asked herself. Another stupid blunder to add to her other blunders—

The patronizing voice inside her head stopped abruptly, the moment Lee realized it was there, taunting her.

A second later, there was a knock at the door, followed by Shane's familiar voice as he identified himself.

Lee stumbled to the door, half-laughing, half-crying with relief. She'd been so certain he was injured or dead!

"You!" she snarled the moment he stepped inside and shut the door behind him. "You left me here to worry myself sick!" She brushed the snow roughly from his shoulders, taking the opportunity to vent some of her pent-up anxiety. "Why were you gone so long? Didn't you know that I would think— that I would think—" She stopped abruptly as he took her hands in his cold ones.

"You're crying."

"I am not!" Lee swiped at her face to wash away the evidence, glaring at him. She wasn't finished with him, not yet. "What do *you* care, anyway? You obviously don't—"

His mouth silenced her shrill words, and melted the anger from her body. She sagged against him. His arms came around her as he moved his mouth a scarce inch to the side to whisper, "I'm sorry I worried you."

Before she could get out a weak protest, his mouth covered hers again, and she was lost. She couldn't fight him, not when he was making her feel this good. In fact, she thought dazedly, it was hard to think at all when she was in Shane's strong arms.

What seemed like hours later, but must have only been moments, he pulled back to look at her. "Do you forgive me?"

"Yes." Now she'd have to decide if she could forgive him for that smug male arrogance in his voice.

Her decision didn't take long. Fast on the heels of her decision to forgive him came a stunning realization.

She was falling in love with Shane Knox.

The knowledge not only terrified her, but evoked a deep, bewildering sadness. She refused to consider what that sadness meant.

They both realized at the same instant that Molly and Buck had fallen silent. Turning quickly, Lee let out a breath of relief to find baby and dog watching them curiously.

Shane chuckled. "If they could talk, we'd be in trouble."

Lee clutched the lapels of his coat and nodded, unwilling to let him go just yet. He smelled of cold and pine and something else that eluded her. Smoke? Was that how he'd stayed warm? Had he stopped to build a fire?

She felt a little foolish for getting so worked up over his absence. Shane knew the area, and was accustomed to the weather.

Reluctantly, she let go of his coat.

****

"Okay, you can come into the kitchen now."

Shane looked up from his kneeling position by the fire, and took in Lee's flushed face. His gaze drifted over her jean-clad figure, pausing when he encountered two white hand prints on her jeans.

Flour, he realized, grinning. Lee had flour on her jeans, and another spot on her chin, and one on her forehead.

When she turned to lead the way, Shane had to

smother a chuckle. She had two white hand prints on her bottom, as well.

In the kitchen, Lee stood aside, tucking her hands inside her jean pockets and ducking her head in a bashful way that Shane found thoroughly arousing.

The table was set with his odd assortment of mismatched plates and flatware. A warped candle graced the center. He sniffed the air, his eyebrow shooting up in surprise. On a hopeful note, he asked, "Meatloaf?"

Lee laughed and snatched the lid from a casserole dish on the table. "Yes, meatloaf. You've got a good nose."

Buck barked and thumped his tail on the floor, hard. Lee smiled down at him. "Yes, Buck, you do, too." An uncertain note crept into her voice. "I just hope it's as good as it smells." She gestured for Shane to take a seat. Molly, for once, was quietly munching on a saltine cracker.

Shane swallowed a suspicious lump in his throat, suddenly very certain he was going to miss the hell out of his ladies.

His ladies.

For now, they were his. Until someone challenged his claim, he would hoard the knowledge like a miser with his gold.

He took a seat and picked up his cloth napkin, trying to recall where she could have found them. When nothing came to mind, he shook his head. What did it matter where the napkins had come from when he had Lee for company and Molly for entertainment?

"I don't know what made me decide I could make a meatloaf," Lee said, serving him a big slice, and taking a smaller one for herself.

Shane watched with great amusement as Lee placed a slice of meatloaf on a third plate and set it on the floor for Buck. She then served him a side of mashed potatoes that smelled heavenly.

"I just found myself putting a little of this and a little of that into the beef, and before I knew it, I had meatloaf." Lee watched him anxiously until he took a bite.

He closed his eyes and smiled as he chewed. "It's the best meatloaf I've ever had." He was telling the truth.

Lee flushed with pleasure and picked up her fork. "Thank you. I—I guess this means I can cook, or at least prepare a meatloaf and mashed potatoes."

Buck had long since wolfed down his share of the bounty and sat waiting for Molly to give him seconds.

But the dog suddenly stiffened and began to growl. His hair rose along his back as he bounded off toward the front door.

Without a word spoken, Shane and Lee rose and followed him. Just as they reached the door, someone knocked.

"Stay behind me," Shane ordered in a low voice. He retrieved his gun and unbolted the door, pulling it open an inch.

When he recognized the two uniformed men standing outside, he relaxed a fraction and put his gun away. He pulled the door open wider so they could come in from the cold. Shane suspected he knew the nature of their visit, but shamelessly found himself hoping he was wrong. He wasn't ready to give up Lee and Molly.

He didn't know if he would *ever* be.

"Penn, Dodd, come inside. You're a long way from home, aren't you?" He glanced at Lee, who looked about as happy as *he* did, and knew she had come to the same conclusion.

Someone must have called the precinct looking for her and Molly.

Knowing he was stalling and that it wouldn't stop the inevitable, Shane took his time introducing his fellow officers to Lee and Molly.

Penn nodded politely at Lee, but remained solemn-faced. Shane noticed that *both* officers looked a little green around the gills. He narrowed his eyes as a growing suspicion took hold. His co-workers wouldn't know he'd become attached to Lee and Molly, so why did they look as if they were about to deliver a death sentence?

Slowly, he asked, "Mind telling me why you're here?"

Penn looked at Dodd, who suddenly found the wall behind Shane interesting. His mouth tightened. "We're on official business, Knox."

Shane lifted a puzzled brow. "Official? I don't understand."

Dodd suddenly came alive. He focused his pained gaze on Shane. "A hiker found a body about two miles from here, in a ravine. He got caught in the storm a few days back, and was going back for his gear."

"He found a *body?*"

"Yeah. It was...Bobby Dillon."

Chapter Ten

Lee didn't think about her motive when she took Shane's hand in a gesture of comfort and support.

There wasn't time to analyze.

She could tell from Shane's expression that it hadn't taken him long to realize he'd come to the wrong conclusion about why the officers were there.

It wasn't to tell them someone was looking for her and Molly.

They thought he had something to do with Bobby Dillon's death.

Shane seemed to want verbal proof, as if a tiny part of him still couldn't quite believe what they were suggesting. "What does finding Bobby Dillon's body have to do with me?"

She winced at his low, furious tone, although she suspected he was more hurt than angry that anyone—especially his co-workers—would believe he was capable of murder.

Dodd glanced at his partner, swallowed visibly, and said, "Everyone knows you and Dillon had several altercations, Knox. The captain just wants to ask you a few questions...before Internal Affairs gets wind of Dillon's death."

"Internal Affairs." Shane repeated the words slowly, still using that gritty tone of disbelief.

Lee's stomach twisted into a knot at the thought of his pain. She couldn't stay quiet. Something wild and bewildering rose inside her. She was stunned to find her voice authoritative and strong as she demanded, "Has anyone confirmed cause of death?"

Penn glanced at her in surprise. "Um, the

coroner thinks he died of a broken neck."

"The coroner *thinks?*" Lee questioned sharply. "You said he was found at the bottom of a ravine."

"That's right, ma'am," Dodd said.

"So he could have slipped and broken his neck."

Dodd looked at Penn again, and Lee wondered if either of them could speak without looking at the other.

"The coroner suspects foul play," Dodd said.

Lee laughed, as if the notion was ridiculous. "Tell me, Officer Dodd, Officer Penn. Did either of you slip coming up that hill to the door?"

Penn finally nodded. "I did, ma'am."

"So you agree that it *is* slippery outside, with the snow packed down and the freezing temperatures."

"Yeah, I guess so."

Since Penn seemed to be the more talkative of the two, she focused a hard, piercing gaze on him. She didn't know where she was getting her courage, but she didn't have time to question it. "And wouldn't you say the same slippery conditions might have existed for Dillon?" She struck a sarcastic, thoughtful pose. "Did either one of you happen to notice the steepness of the ravine where Dillon was found?"

"Yes, ma'am."

"And in your opinion, Officer Penn, would you say it was steeper than the incline outside this cabin?"

Penn cleared his throat, staring at Shane as he answered Lee. "Yes."

Lee's tone matched the frigid temperature outside. "I think the coroner may have been a little too hasty with his suspicions, don't you?"

"Maybe, but it's not really up to me—"

"Weren't you one of the officers on the scene?" Lee cut in sharply.

"Yes, ma'am, but the captain said Knox was

overheard threatening Dillon just yesterday."

Beside her, Lee felt Shane stiffen. Was he reacting because they told the truth about his threat, or was he as surprised by her fierce defense as *she* was?

She gave her head an incredulous shake, allowing a cynical smile to curve her lips. "The captain is calling Shane in for questioning on the basis of a little office *gossip?*" Turning to Shane, she let go of his hand and folded her arms over her chest. "You don't have to go. They have absolutely *no* valid, legal reason to question you. Why, they haven't even performed an autopsy!"

Shane stared at her, his amazement obvious. He seemed robbed of the ability to speak.

"Look, ma'am," Penn said, beginning to sound agitated. "If you can confirm that he was here at the cabin with you all day long, then we can go back and tell the captain he has an airtight alibi."

For the first time since Lee sprang to Shane's defense, she hesitated. The woman in her wanted to boldly lie and claim Shane had been with her all day; the lawyer—

Oh, God. The lawyer—

Could it be true? She gulped air into her lungs and trampled ruthlessly on her dismaying discovery. Time enough later to consider what it meant and *why* it dismayed her. Right now, she faced a moral dilemma.

If she lied for Shane, she would not only compromise her integrity, she might also re-enforce his belief that all lawyers were the same lying, greedy pond scum.

If she told the truth, she might seal his fate. Without an alibi, and with the past altercations with Dillon, he might very well end up with life in prison.

She did not, even for a second, consider that Shane might be capable of murder.

Looking at him, she realized she would get no help there. He stared back at her, his dark eyes without expression. Without a single hint of what he wanted her to do.

As if he were waiting, she thought. Waiting in judgment?

In the end, there was only one choice she could live with.

Her throat burned as she squared her shoulders and said, "No, I can't confirm he was here all day. Did the coroner confirm time of death?"

Penn shook his head. "No. In these frigid conditions, I think it's difficult to tell."

The knowledge cheered Lee, because she knew—without fully understanding *how* she knew—that this uncertainty would be an asset in her defense of Shane.

To Shane, she said, "I think you should make them come back with a warrant. That would give you time to obtain legal counsel before you go in."

His expression remained frustratingly bland as he said softly, "I think I've found my legal counsel, don't you?"

Lee's first instinct was to deny his charge. Loudly and vehemently. By his own admission, Shane mistrusted and detested lawyers in any shape, form, or fashion.

What if he was right, and she was one of *them?*

Would he detest *her?*

****

She was close to regaining her memory.

Shane sensed it, and the knowledge terrified him, more so than the prospect of being charged with murder.

Yet he could do nothing, say nothing. Not now, with Penn and Dodd getting antsy to return to the precinct and away from this barracuda of a lawyer.

The thought almost made him smile, but he

refrained. He suspected Lee's outward strength was a front. Inwardly, she was probably just as frightened by today's revelations as *he* was, if not more so.

Anything he said or did could cause a setback, and although a selfish part of him *wanted* to keep her in the dark, he knew she needed to remember.

He didn't want her to be alone when she did.

Making a decision, he looked at Penn. "Lee and I will follow you back to town, okay? I don't want to leave her and the baby alone."

Dodd looked relieved, and Penn nodded, glancing behind him at the baby and Buck, who had been silently watching the exchange. "I guess that will be all right. I don't reckon you plan on running."

"He has no reason to run," Lee snapped, her violet eyes flashing at the uneasy officers. "So get that through your heads. Shane is not a murderer, and *everyone* is innocent until proven guilty. It's the law."

Hastily, Penn reached for the door. "We'll just wait in the car, Knox."

Despite the direness of the situation, Shane had to fight another smile at their hasty retreat. He found himself anticipating the captain's reaction to Lee.

"Shane—" Lee began.

Shane put a finger to her lips, keeping his expression blank. "We'll talk about it later, okay? Why don't you get Molly into her snowsuit while I pack the diaper bag."

When she was out of earshot, he smiled, imagining Dodd and Penn's expressions if he'd mentioned packing a diaper bag in front of them. As for Dillon's death, he couldn't say he was sorry to hear the news. The world would be a safer place for women without the man.

It would be hard to keep that opinion to himself,

he thought, preparing two bottles of formula and taking an extra can as a precaution. But he knew he should make an effort, especially if he had to talk to Internal Affairs. Answering direct questions was one thing; expressing his opinion without being asked was another.

He was almost certain Lee would agree.

Lee...Shane paused with his hand in the box of disposable diapers, disconcerted by the possibility that her name could be Susan or Greta, something not even remotely close Lee. Would he be able to make the switch in his mind, as well as in his speech?

And then he remembered that it wouldn't matter. When she regained her memory, she would be going home, probably back to Texas, as the PT Cruiser's license plate indicated.

Shane's hand mangled a diaper as he pictured a tall, handsome Texan enfolding her in his arms. Whoever the man was in Lee's life, he couldn't possibly love her as much as *Shane* did.

"Son of a..." Shane swallowed the rest of the curse and stuffed a handful of diapers into the diaper bag, zipped it, then tossed it over his shoulder.

He loved Lee. He didn't care if she was a lawyer or a hairdresser. He didn't care if she had one child or ten.

He didn't give a great damn if she was married, or not. Her marital status couldn't stop him from loving her.

But loving her didn't change the situation, he mused darkly. She was married to someone else, and the moment she remembered her other life, she would be lost to him.

And Molly, too.

"I'm going to warm up the Jeep," he growled at Lee as she emerged from the bedroom with a bundled Molly on her hip. He caught her surprised look, but didn't pause to explain his sudden mood change. Let her think it was because he was upset over the fact that everyone in Asheville was probably speculating on just how he thought he could get away with murder.

He didn't kill Bobby Dillon, but he couldn't say that he hadn't fantasized about it—not once, but several times. Hell, truth be told, he most likely wasn't the *only* one who had dreamed of putting the man out of his misery.

Sandra Dillon's father, for instance. Or either of her two brothers. They had all expressed their outrage and disgust over the many beatings the woman had received while married to Dillon. When Dillon had walked, they'd muttered their share of threats, as well. He wondered if anyone would remember.

Shane cast a baleful glance at the starless sky as he tromped to the Jeep. Lee had been right about the slippery surface. Sleet mixed with snow on top of snow had created a hazard for anyone brave enough to venture out. He had known this from the moment he stepped foot outside early this morning.

Now that it was dark again, the danger had increased.

When the Jeep's heater had taken the chill from the interior, Shane returned to the house to help Lee with Molly. Molly wasn't exactly a featherweight, and he didn't want to risk an accident.

Moments later, they were ready to go. Molly and Buck were in the back—Molly in her car seat and bundled so warmly, she couldn't move. Lee clipped on her seat belt and Shane did the same.

Yesterday, Shane had mapped out the road with his Jeep, and today the patrol vehicle had redefined the ruts, so the going this time was a lot easier.

Shane was keenly aware of Lee's mysterious

silence, and of Molly's unintelligible jabbering in the back seat. The wind rocked the Jeep on occasion as they followed the taillights of the patrol car to the outer road leading to the interstate. Once there, the roads were clear and dry and both vehicles were able to pick up speed.

Thirty minutes into the ride, Lee finally spoke. "Did you run into Dillon today?"

The Jeep swerved sharply to avoid a boulder of packed, dirty snow left behind by the snowplows. Shane swallowed a curse at her question and managed to answer calmly, "I told you I didn't see him."

"And you weren't just saying that to keep me from worrying?"

His mouth tightened. "I didn't lie just to keep you from worrying."

"It wouldn't really be a lie—"

"I didn't lie!" he snapped, darting a quick, angry glance her way. She had no idea how much her suspicion hurt. Or did she?

She glanced into the back seat to check on Molly, then turned back to face the windshield. "I want you to tell me your every move from the time you left the cabin to the time you returned."

"There's a reason for this interrogation?"

"Yes."

"And you'll tell me...when?" he drawled bitingly. From the corner of his eye, he saw her glance at him, then quickly look away. It was enough time for him to notice she was biting her bottom lip.

"When I figure out what I'm doing, I'll let you know."

Shane felt a queer lurch in his belly. She sounded oddly shaky, reminding him that she wasn't as tough as she sometimes acted. "When I left the cabin, I followed Dillon's tracks."

"With the way the wind's blowing the snow

around, they weren't covered?"

"Despite the fact that my old man wasn't around much, he did teach me a few things. I know how to track a man." He flipped the heater fan down a notch; he didn't want to make Molly uncomfortable. Grimly, he continued, "I found Dillon's campfire, still warm, not more than a mile north of the cabin."

"How do you know it was Dillon's?"

"Nobody lives within ten miles of my cabin, Lee. *That's* how I knew it was Dillon's."

"Oh. What did you do after that?"

"I stoked the fire and got myself warm. Then I made certain the fire was out before continuing to track him. I lost his trail more than once, but managed to pick it back up again. The trail led me to the road at the bottom of the mountain." Shane hesitated, knowing she was going to be furious that he didn't tell her. "I found his truck."

She didn't disappoint him.

"You didn't tell me."

"No, I didn't."

"Protecting me, Shane?"

"Maybe I just didn't see any reason to tell you."

"Protecting me," she repeated, angling her chin in a way that was both endearing and familiar. "You must think I'm helpless." With a hint of self-derision, she added softly, "But then, I guess I've given you no reason to think otherwise."

"I know you're not helpless."

She ignored his protest. "Tell me the rest, and don't leave out any details."

"After I found the truck, I followed his tracks back up the mountain, into the woods heading in the direction of the cabin again." Shane's hands tightened on the steering wheel in anticipation of her response. "About an hour into his new trail, I came upon a pregnant doe he'd shot."

"Oh, God," Lee muttered, closing her eyes. She

let out a disgusted breath. "It's not hunting season, is it?"

"No. I think he shot her just for the fun of it. He left her there for the coyotes to find." He saw no reason to add that the doe had still been alive and suffering, and that he'd had to put her out of her misery. Lee had enough to deal with. "Farther along the trail, I found an empty whiskey bottle. That's when I decided to return to the cabin." He'd known he was courting trouble tracking Dillon in the first place. The whiskey bottle had prompted his common sense into play.

"So you never actually *saw* Dillon."

It wasn't a question, so Shane didn't bother answering. "Are you ready to tell me what this is all about?" *How much had she remembered?* He didn't realize he was holding is breath until his lungs began to cry out for air.

"I—I think I needed to know so I could prepare a defense on your behalf," she said slowly, uncertainly.

"You've remembered who you are?" Shane swallowed hard and braced himself for her answer. His heart was pounding.

He was terrified.

Chapter Eleven

Molly had fallen asleep, and so had Buck. It was so quiet inside the Jeep, Lee could hear herself breathing.

Fast. Hard. Gulping at the air like a person with asthma.

And Shane was so quiet, she didn't think *he* was breathing at all. She glanced at her hands folded in her lap, belatedly realizing she'd forgotten her gloves.

"Lee?"

She jumped at his soft prompt, gathering her scattered thoughts. "To answer your question, no. I haven't remembered *who* am. Just—just maybe *what* I am. My head is filled with legal mumble jumble, so much that I'm fairly certain I'm either a lawyer, or I'm training to be one." She touched the freckles on her face, then spread her hands to indicate her jean-clad figure, not bothering to hide her bewilderment. "I know I don't look like a lawyer—"

"I don't have any hang-ups about the way you look," Shane interjected. "But it's obvious *you* do. I think someone in your life gave you a hard time about it. Do you remember anything else?"

She shook her head and sighed. "It's weird, I know, but I'm not even certain I'm a lawyer."

"If you're not," Shane said with a hint of amusement, "Then you do a damned good job imitating one."

"Maybe I watched a lot of *Law and Order*."

"Maybe, but I don't think you got your skills

from watching television."

She kept waiting for his voice to thicken with disappointment or disgust or both. What was he really thinking about her possible discovery? That he wished he'd left her in that PT Cruiser to freeze? That he wished he'd never kissed her? If *he* wasn't so good at hiding his feelings, maybe she wouldn't be driving herself insane wondering!

"Maybe the reason I can't remember is because I'm one of those sleazy lawyers you detest," she suggested boldly. "Maybe I'm ashamed of my profession."

He slanted her an enigmatic look. "You could never be sleazy, Lee."

She flushed at his compliment, although she noticed he didn't deny that the rest might be true. "Whether I'm a real lawyer or not, I'd like to be present when you talk to the captain."

He nodded. "Okay."

Okay? Lee found herself surprised and pleased by his easy acceptance of her offer. Or was he just humoring her? Did he truly believe she could help him?

Her emotions made an about-face as self-doubt and terror crept in. What if she failed him? What if she unwittingly made things worse? What if she forgot as suddenly as she had remembered?

She tried to hide her panic as she said, "I—I think maybe I was a little too hasty in offering—"

"Oh, no you don't. You're not chickening out on me now, Lee. In fact, there's no time. We're here."

With a start, she realized they'd left the interstate and were now driving in downtown Asheville. As her mind whirled with dread and confusion, Shane pulled into a parking spot reserved for police cars and cut the engine.

"I'll get Molly. Buck, as much as I'd like to see the captain have a sneezing fit, I guess you'd better sit this one out." He glanced at Lee. "The captain's allergic to dogs."

He got out of the Jeep and opened the back door, reaching for Molly, who had awakened the moment Shane cut the engine. "Let's hope he likes kids," Lee muttered, letting herself out and coming around to where Shane stood with Molly.

Shane smiled. "He has seven kids of his own, so he'd *better* like them."

"Seven?" Lee widened her eyes at him. "I thought police captains were married to their jobs."

"Not this one, although he's on his third marriage. Come on. Let's get Molly out of this wind."

Dodd and Penn were waiting just inside the door. They fell into step beside her and Shane as they wound their way through the noisy police station. Molly's eyes were big round saucers, taking in their colorful surroundings.

Watching her wondrous face, Lee felt a familiar pang of guilt, made even stronger by her recent breakthrough. How could she remember legal technicalities, but not her own baby? Was she not only a sleazy lawyer, but a bad mother? Could she bear to see Shane's possessive, desiring gaze turn to disgust and anger?

She could see the captain through the glass windows of his office before they reached him. He was a balding man who looked to be in his early forties, tall and thin, wearing striped suspenders he undoubtedly needed. He was talking on the phone when they entered.

He glanced up, narrowed his eyes, and promptly hung up the phone. Whoever he'd been talking to, Lee thought with a nervous swallow, hadn't gotten so much as a bye or see ya later.

The captain propped his hands on his slim hips and regarded Shane and Molly, then Lee. When he finished his inspection, he waved Dodd and Penn out, then turned back to Shane and lifted his brows.

"Did I miss your wedding—*and* the birth of your first child?"

Shane's expression remained stony. Good for him, Lee thought, standing straight and proud beside him. She was relieved to feel that odd, defensive need rising inside her.

"No, you didn't," Shane said. He jerked his chin at Lee. "This is Lee, and this is Molly. What did you want to talk to me about?"

"Have a seat."

Lee offered to take Molly, but Molly clung tightly to Shane's neck, rejecting her. Shane shook his head and took a seat in front of the desk. Lee started to do the same, but hesitated when she noticed the captain showed no signs of sitting. *It's a power play,* she thought, startled by the realization. She remained standing.

The captain didn't seem to notice her decision. "You know by now that Dillon's dead," he told Shane. "And *I* know he was threatening to get even with you. Thought he might have paid you a visit."

Shane adjusted Molly on his lap, smiling down at her. The moment he looked at the captain again, his smile disappeared. "If that's all you wanted to know, you could have had Dodd or Penn ask me. What you really want to know, Captain Maynard, is whether I had anything to do with Dillon's death."

"Did you?"

"No."

"Haven't you thought about it, Knox?"

Lee stepped forward. "You don't have to answer that, Shane. In fact, I advise you not to."

"Yes," Shane said, holding the captain's gaze and ignoring Lee. "And I'm not the only one."

"We both know you've been under a lot of stress...since Sandra Dillon's death. Is it possible—"

This time, Lee stepped in front of Shane,

effectively breaking eye-contact. She knew this line of questioning was hurting Shane, even if the captain didn't. Looking the captain square in the eye, she ordered Shane, "Don't say another word."

Captain Maynard's face turned an ugly shade of pink. "Listen, little lady, you'd better—"

"I'm here in Shane's defense, and you're not *my* boss, so you can save your breath, Captain. I'm not easily frightened." She tensed, half-expecting Shane to burst out laughing at her obvious lie. But strangely enough, she no longer felt frightened or nervous.

In fact, she felt...*powerful*. And she suddenly, instinctively knew why.

She had the law on her side.

Her chin edged outward another notch. In response, the captain's eyes narrowed slightly. "Shane says he didn't kill Dillon. Either arrest him, or stop harassing him."

"I'm his captain. I can ask him any damn thing I want." A muscle began to tick in the captain's jaw, betraying his anger.

"The fact that Shane's under your supervision doesn't give you the right to accuse him of murder."

"Internal Affairs will be a lot tougher."

"Hopefully," Lee shot back, "They'll have a lot more to go on than *you* do. Otherwise, why would they get involved?" She let out a scornful little snort. "I doubt Internal Affairs listens to office gossip."

In a low, barely controlled voice, the captain told her, "He hit Dillon during an arrest. Everyone in town knows that. They'll be expecting me to question him."

"He hit Dillon in self-defense. Everyone who knows *Dillon* should know that." She leaned forward. "As his captain, *you* should know that Shane is not capable of murder."

Shane's hand landed on her hip. He gently

pushed her aside, then handed Molly to her. "Wait outside with Molly. I want to talk to the captain."

"But—"

"Go."

Sensing his resolve, Lee snapped her mouth shut and left the office with Molly. Outside the closed door, she turned around to watch them through the glass. Was she actually thinking about reading their lips? she wondered, amazed at her temerity.

"So, you're the reason my partner's been so flustered," a deep voice said from behind her.

Lee whirled around, ready and willing to go to bat for Shane again with this new adversary.

Then she realized what he'd said, at the same instant taking in the tall, distinguished Native American. His long, gray-streaked braids in no way detracted from his rugged masculinity.

"I'm Kyle Grayfeather."

"You're Shane's partner," she blurted out. Molly let out a shriek and reached for one of his braids.

To Lee's amazement, Kyle leaned forward so Molly could wrap her chubby fingers around one. He grinned at Lee.

"Kids seem to have a strange fascination for my hair," he confessed. "I have two daughters. They fight over who will braid my hair."

Molly, oblivious to the two adults, reached out with her other hand to snag the second braid. She caught it, laughing joyously, and yanked him forward.

Lee found herself nose to nose with Kyle. She flushed and tried to draw back, but Molly kept a strangle-hold on the braids. "I'm—I'm sorry—"

Kyle solved the problem by taking Molly from her, chuckling over Lee's embarrassment. "Can I offer you some coffee?" His voice danced a bit as Molly gleefully yanked and pulled on his braids.

She shook her head, glancing back at the arguing men behind the glass. "Shane might need me."

He laughed outright. "Knox never needs anyone." Her dismay must have been evident, for he shrugged and added, "Until now, anyway. The captain knows he didn't kill Dillon. He's just preparing Shane for Internal Affairs. He hates those guys with a passion."

His words failed to comfort Lee. She'd spoken with the captain, and she couldn't agree with Kyle. "If the captain believes he's innocent, he has a funny way of showing it."

"If my partner was involved, then I believe it was an accident."

Lee stiffened at his suggestion. "If Shane knows anything about Dillon's death, why wouldn't he say so?"

Kyle's black brow rose as he waited for her to come to her own conclusion.

It didn't take long. Lee shook her head. "No, no. You're wrong. Even if Shane feared nobody would believe him, he wouldn't lie. Not to me."

His other brow joined the first, emphasizing his surprise. "You've known him how many days?"

"None of your damn business," Shane said pleasantly, coming up beside Lee. "Why don't you pick on someone your own size, Grayfeather?"

The moment Molly caught sight of Shane, she let go of Kyle's braids and leaped in Shane's direction. Shane caught her deftly up into his arms. He settled her to one side and snaked a possessive arm around Lee's waist.

She flushed beneath Kyle's astute gaze. She glanced at Shane to find him giving his partner a long, hard look. His hand tightened at her waist.

"You believe I had something to do with Dillon's death?" Shane asked softly, without inflection.

If the notion hurt, Lee knew that Kyle would never know. Shane Knox was a proud man.

Kyle's dark, steady gaze never wavered. "I don't believe you are capable of murder."

"Glad to hear it."

Lee felt his hand relax slightly, and she relaxed with him. They both stiffened again at Kyle's next statement.

"I have news for you on that matter we discussed. The fax came in this morning."

She knew Kyle could have been talking about anything, but she instinctively sensed it was about her and Molly. Her mouth went dry.

Silently, they followed Kyle back to his desk. He sorted through a pile of stacked papers, withdrew a sheet, and handed it to Shane.

"It came from the Galveston office."

Shane held it out of Molly's reach so they could read it together.

The moment Lee saw the name Brandon Lynch, she felt a sharp pain behind her eyes. She swayed, clutching Shane's arm to steady herself as she read the missing person's report.

Brandon Lynch was looking for a woman fitting her description, and a little girl named Molly.

Her name, the official-looking paper said, was Leandra DeHart. Not Leandra Lynch, but Leandra *DeHart*.

What did it mean? If Brandon Lynch was her husband, why did she have a different last name? Was she one of those liberated women who insisted on keeping their own name when they married?

"I've already notified the Galveston office," Kyle said. "Lynch will be here in the morning."

Shane shot him a cold look. "You were going to bring him to the cabin without warning me?"

Kyle didn't look the least perturbed by Shane's scowling face. "Maybe now you'll think about getting

125

Sheridon Smythe

a cell phone."

Molly finally got her hands on the paper, ripping it down the middle. It was no less than Lee felt like doing, and she didn't have a clue why.

Panic sank its ugly claws into her belly. *Why was she afraid?* Why did the idea of meeting someone from her past terrify her? Why didn't she *feel* married?

Her gaze slid to Shane, and she knew by the way his eyes darkened to black that he read the fear in her eyes.

His jaw clacked shut. He shoved what was left of the paper onto Kyle's desk. "I'll bring them back in the morning. Tell—tell Lynch to wait here." He shifted Molly in his arms. "Can I borrow your cell phone?"

Kyle shrugged and pulled the compact phone from a small leather case hooked to his belt. "It's about time you got with the program, partner. Anything else?"

"Yeah. I want a background check on Brandon Lynch. Anything you can find."

"You got it."

"Call me when you get it."

"Will do, partner."

With a sense of doom weighting her shoulders, Lee took the hand Shane offered.

They looked like an ordinary family, she thought as they left the precinct.

If only...

****

Shane cursed himself for not thinking to check on Lynch before now. Why hadn't he? Had he been so distracted by Lee and Molly that he'd lost his edge?

He couldn't forget the look of absolute terror on Lee's face when she'd read the report.

It convinced him that he'd been right about Lee

126

being a runaway wife, and wives usually didn't run away without a damn good reason.

Especially with a baby.

He gunned the engine and shot out of the parking lot before he remembered his precious cargo. Forcing himself to slow down, he headed for the interstate and home.

Home.

With Lee and Molly.

One last time.

"What do you think it means?" Lee asked quietly.

The moment he'd merged safely into the sporadic traffic, Shane took a good look at her.

She looked pale and shaken, and was it any wonder? She'd had one shock after another. He knew she was a strong woman, but how much could any one person take without cracking?

Despite his determination to protect her, fear roughened his voice. "It means that a man named Brandon Lynch is looking for you...and Molly."

"No, not that. The part about my name. I don't have his last name. I don't *feel* like he's my husband."

His heart stuttered, then leaped shamelessly with a wild hope that was quickly squashed by the cold, hateful voice of reason. "If you didn't want to be found, chances are you wouldn't be using your married name. DeHart could be your maiden name."

She let out a great sigh that made him want to pull over and take her into his arms.

"Maybe I keep thinking I can't be married because that's what we want to—want *I* want to think."

Shane started to correct her, to tell her that he wanted it as desperately as she did. But he couldn't. If she was someone's wife, then it would be hard enough without adding his declaration of love.

"I'm scared," she whispered, clutching her stomach as if she were about to be sick.

"Hell," he said, swerving to the shoulder of the road and grinding the Jeep to a halt. Buck barked a protest as he lost his balance on the seat and slid to the floor. "If you don't remember this man, you don't have to go with him. You can stay with me." Maybe it wasn't the wisest thing to say, or the wisest choice to make, but he meant every damned word of it.

Slowly, she looked at him, her eyes wide with a heart-tugging fear that made his protective instincts clamor.

"Are—are you sure? I mean, we've imposed on you enough."

"You haven't imposed." He had to grip the wheel to keep from reaching out to her. But he had to be strong, for both of them. Taking her in his arms right now would be too risky.

Telling her that he loved her would be emotional suicide.

"Shane, I—I want you to know that I—"

The ringing of the cell phone in his coat pocket shattered the moment. Shane scowled, cursing that single, brain-dead moment when he'd asked for the damn thing. He fumbled in his pockets until his hand closed over the cold plastic.

As he was jerking it free, he remembered why he'd borrowed it in the first place.

His somber gaze met Lee's apprehensive one as he flipped it open and barked his name into the receiver.

Chapter Twelve

Shane had said she didn't have to go.

It was those words Lee concentrated on as she waited for Shane to finish his conversation with his partner.

She knew she should be overjoyed to find out her real name. She knew that somewhere, deep inside, she should be happy to discover she and Molly hadn't just dropped from the sky in the midst of a freak blizzard, that someone out there loved them and had been searching for them.

The logical side—and she did have a logical side—told her she should be thrilled to find out she knew a lot about the law, indicating a sharp mind and a possible career that should make any woman proud.

Instead, she felt ashamed, bewildered, and scared.

And Shane seemed to understand.

She jumped as he viciously snapped the phone shut. He shoved it back into his pocket and looked at her, his expression shadowed and unreadable.

"Grayfeather called to tell me his cell phone would only stay charged another three hours if I left it on. Since I don't have the charger, I have to turn it off and only turn it on when I get ready to call him." Shane gazed at the windshield. "He said he should have information about Lynch by midnight tonight."

Lee gave her lips a nervous swipe with her tongue. *He looked and sounded so tense.*

That made two of them!

"He—he seems like a good friend."

129

Shane's laugh held little humor. "He thought I had something to do with Dillon's fall."

She felt compelled to defend his partner, who hadn't minded Molly's attempt to yank his braids from his scalp. "I don't think he believes you killed him, Shane. I think he's afraid you might have scuffled with him, and that Dillon might have fallen."

He turned a stony expression her way. Very softly, he asked her, "Is that what *you* think, Lee?"

"I never doubted your story."

Flipping on his turn signal, he checked his mirrors as he waited for a safe gap in the traffic. "Grayfeather's checking on the autopsy report. They'll be doing a tissue analysis to see how long he's been...frozen."

"Glee!" Molly chirped from the back seat. She kicked her feet against the car seat and clapped her hands. "Glee! Glee!"

"Okay, honey," Shane said to Molly, "I'm going."

It was amazing, Lee thought, how his voice changed when he talked to Molly. "You should have children," Lee blurted out.

Shane smiled grimly. "My ex-wife would have disagreed with you."

"Maybe she didn't know you."

"And you think that you do?" he countered softly.

Lee felt a burst of irritation at his condescending tone. It was obvious he was trying to push her away. "I know you're great with Molly. I know you would probably die for her, if it came down to it. I also know you're going to miss her."

"Very astute, counselor," he drawled.

She flushed, reminding herself that he was simply trying to prepare her for the inevitable break. "I'm stronger than I look, you know."

He cast her an appraising look that made her

blush even harder. "Evidently."

"Why are you being so nasty?" she challenged.

"I'm trying to prepare you."

She'd known that much, hadn't she? "For what?"

"For whatever."

"You still think I was running away from something, or someone?"

"Don't you?"

"I don't know what to think," she said honestly. "When I saw Brandon Lynch's name on that fax, I felt scared. No, not scared, exactly." She frowned. "It was more like *dismayed,* as if I had disappointed someone, and didn't want to face them."

"Try not to stress yourself."

"But I *want* to remember!" She made a fist and punched her knee with it. Her frustration was so great she wanted to scream, and would have, if she wasn't afraid she'd scare Molly. "I want to remember before I have to face *him.*" Her voice sank to a miserable whisper. "What if I don't remember after I've seen him face to face? What then?"

"I told you that you didn't have to go with him."

"But I do, don't I? If I'm his wife, and Molly's his daughter, then I have to go. I can't stay with you forever."

If only she could, she thought, fighting the urge to cry. Crying would accomplish nothing, and might upset Molly. As subtly as she could, she turned her face to the passenger window and stuffed her fist into her mouth.

How could she leave Shane?

****

Once inside the cabin, Lee felt a sense of peace steal over her. She knew it was just because she couldn't remember another home, another place, yet she hugged that peaceful feeling to her breast like a hard-won gold medal.

Shane was another reason this felt like home,

she mused, watching him as he removed Molly's snowsuit and laid the sleeping baby on the bed. He handled her as if she was made of glass, and his expression as he gazed down at her was worth a thousand words.

He loved Molly, she realized, not truly surprised by the knowledge, but pleased nonetheless. But then, who *wouldn't* love Molly?

They tip-toed from the room and went to the kitchen. Lee pulled two packages of instant hot chocolate from the pantry and held them up in a silent question. He nodded, his expression solemn.

Her hands shook as she heated the water. This time tomorrow night, she might be in another kitchen in another state, boiling water for her husband's cocoa, or tea. Or did he drink coffee?

Was he nice? Would she ever catch him looking at her with undisguised yearning, as Shane did? Did he laugh gently at her clumsy ways, or did he ridicule her?

Did she love him? And how could she, when she loved Shane so much it hurt to think of never seeing him again?

Wordlessly, Shane moved beside her, taking the envelopes of cocoa from her nerveless fingers. He ripped the packages open and dumped the contents into the two coffee cups she'd taken from the cabinet above the sink.

She watched, dazed, as he poured the boiling water into the cups.

"Let's go sit by the fire," he said, his voice so soft and gentle it brought instant tears to her eyes.

Did he pity her, then? she wondered.

She took a deep, shaky breath and followed him into the living room. He set her cocoa down on the end table, then took the chair, leaving her favorite corner of the sofa open.

Polite. Considerate.

Sexy. Strong.

Molly adored him. Did she adore her own father as much? Would she miss Shane? She would, Lee knew. Just as *she* would. So very, very much.

At least she would have her memories.

But Lee wanted more. Would he give it? Did she dare ask for more? Curling up on the couch, she tucked her legs under her and stared at the fire, painfully aware of Shane watching her.

He was so close, yet beneath the tension that thrummed strongly between them, she sensed a restraint in him that hadn't been there before tonight.

She turned the wedding band on her finger, wishing she had the guts to rip it off and toss it into the fire. Just for one night, she wanted to be free to love Shane and be loved by Shane.

She wanted to forget not only the fact that she couldn't remember her previous life. She wanted to forget that after tonight, she wouldn't see Shane again.

Possibly ever.

The thought was almost too much to bear.

"It's nearly midnight," he said, his voice low and rough, as if he, too, had been thinking thoughts he shouldn't. "I should call Grayfeather, see what he found out."

Her stomach lurched, then settled. She bit her lip hard enough to bring blood, and said nothing. If she opened her mouth, she might beg him to forget about the call, to forget about Brandon Lynch and the wedding band on her finger.

Just for one night.

He got up and retrieved the cell phone from his coat pocket, then returned to his chair to make the call.

Neither seemed capable of looking at the other as he waited for Grayfeather to answer.

"Knox, here."

She mangled her fingers until they burned, turning the ring around and around, staring into the fire as she listened to Shane's side of the conversation.

"Nothing at all?" Shane asked.

She thought he sounded both relieved *and* frustrated.

"Yeah, I owe you one. Thanks. Bye."

Shane sighed, setting the phone on the end table. "He found an address on Lynch, but Lynch apparently doesn't have a record. He sweet-talked someone from the Galveston office into sending a car out to his last known address."

Lee tensed and closed her eyes, waiting for the verdict.

"It appears the house is empty. There's a realtor sign on the front lawn."

Shock hummed along her taut nerve-endings. She licked her dry lips, forcing herself to look into his handsome, familiar face. His eyes were black and fathomless. "That's—that's it? That's all he found?" Her voice was nothing more than a hoarse croak.

Shane's mouth tightened perceptibly. "That's it. We didn't gain any ground, did we?"

"No." She was so relieved, she felt faint. "Which means there's still a chance..." Her voice wavered as her gaze locked with his.

Very softly, Shane said, "That you aren't married? That Brandon Lynch doesn't exist? You have to face facts, Lee. Whoever Lynch is, he isn't just going to forget about you and Molly."

His face blurred as tears filled her eyes. "I—I can't stand the thought of leaving here...leaving *you.*"

With a crooked smile, he slipped to his knees before her and took her cold hands in his big, warm ones. "A shrink would probably tell you that you're feeling this way because this place—*me*—is all you know right now."

But Lee was shaking her head before he could finish, tears trekking down her face and spilling from her chin onto their entangled hands. "He'd be wrong! He'd be very wrong. I don't want to leave because—because I—"

Shane put a finger to her lips, his expression agonized. "Don't say it, Lee. You don't know what you're saying."

She jerked her hands free, glaring at him. "Don't tell me what I feel! I *know* what I feel, and I—I—"

His mouth smothered her dangerous confession, the heat of his desire blazing as hot as the fire at his back. When they came up for air, Lee framed his face with her palms and forced him to look into her eyes.

"I love you," she whispered, her voice breaking.

He kissed the tears from her cheeks, her eyes, and finally her mouth again, pulling her onto the floor with him. Lee went willingly. She took his hand and placed it against her breast, aching for his touch. He moaned against her mouth, thrusting his tongue inside to stoke the fires even brighter.

Together, they fumbled with the buttons on her blouse, yanking it free of her jeans. When she was finally bare to his gaze, he stared at her a long moment, his expression a mixture of raw desire and wonderment.

He cupped her small, firm breasts in both hands. "You're perfect," he whispered, bending to taste her straining peaks.

Lee felt the tugging of his mouth clear to her toes. She was breathing in quick, harsh gasps, wanting to taste him as he was tasting her. She pushed his shirt aside and began raining kisses against his neck, working her way across his chest to his flat nipple.

He groaned and grabbed her face, moving her back to his mouth.

There was something wild and different about this kiss, Lee thought, feeling as if she was breaking apart. She wanted him naked against her, moving inside her. She wanted to know Shane fully as a woman knows her husband.

She tossed the slender thread of her pride aside and pulled back, begging him with her eyes and her heart, and finally, with her voice. "Make love to me, Shane! Give me something to remember—"

"Hell," he growled roughly, then surprised her by thrusting her away. He staggered to his feet, staring down at her as he ran a trembling hand through his hair.

His breathing was ragged and harsh.

"I can't, Lee. I can't do this to you."

Lee was still caught in a thick fog of need and desire. Her body cried out for his touch, for his possession. Her mouth throbbed from his kisses. *What was he saying?*

She reached out to him, but he stepped away.

His words finally sank in, but it was the tortured resolve on his face that got through to her. Slowly, she rose, using the couch for support until she had regained her footing and stood before him.

"I shouldn't have let it go this far," he added in a low voice filled with regret. "I don't want you to remember me like this, as the man who took advantage of your memory loss. I don't want you to hate me, Leandra."

It was the first time he'd used her real name, and Lee felt as if he'd slapped her. Her head actually jerked back as if an invisible hand had smacked her on the cheek. "I could never hate you," she whispered. And because she didn't want him to see how badly he'd wounded her with his rejection, she turned and ran for the bedroom.

"Lee!"

She heard him calling, recognized the agony and frustration in his voice, but she didn't stop until the door was safely shut behind her.

Aching and quivering with need, she sank to the cold floor and pulled her knees to her chest.

Silently, she cried.

****

From her view in the passenger seat of Shane's Jeep, Lee scanned the precinct parking lot, searching for a familiar vehicle.

There were quite a few civilian cars among the numerous squad cars, but not a single one tickled her memory.

She'd awakened to the cold light of dawn, her eyes gritty and sore, her throat scratchy and dry, and her memory as useless as ever.

That left plenty of room for the new memories, and even those she wished she could forget. Had she truly thrown herself into Shane's arms and begged him to make love to her?

Heat rushed into her face as she recalled his rejection, although the maddeningly logical side of her brain reasoned that Shane had been justified in putting a halt to their love-making.

He didn't really know her, or her background. She could be a member of the mafia, or a woman madly in love with a husband she temporarily couldn't remember.

Shane was right. It *was* possible she would have regretted it if things had progressed between them.

But Lee didn't really believe that. In her heart, with her very soul, she felt connected to Shane, and she didn't think a husband was going to change that.

It sounded silly and ruthless when she thought about it in those harsh terms, she mused, aware of the ticking of the motor and the sound of Shane's shallow breathing beside her.

"Are you ready?"

She jumped at his question. Taking a deep breath, she grabbed the door handle and gave it a yank. "Let's get this over with," she said, stepping out onto the slushy parking lot. The temperatures had risen above freezing for the first time in five days.

Reluctantly, she fell into step beside Shane, who was carrying a sleepy-eyed Molly. Molly grinned at her, and Lee forced herself to smile back.

The closer they came to the entrance, the more nervous Lee felt.

It was early, yet the precinct was in full swing. Half the people were shouting into their phones, Lee noted as they made their way through the noisy building. The other half were eating doughnuts and drinking coffee, while they took information.

Grayfeather was alone at his desk. Lee's knees nearly buckled with relief. A wild hope gripped her. Had Lynch decided not to come?

"You just missed him," Grayfeather said, apparently reading her expression. "They went to get a cup of coffee."

So, her husband drank coffee. The knowledge meant nothing to Lee.

Shane's partner spent a few moments reacquainting himself with Molly, who seemed delighted to see him again. Finally, he said to Shane, "The captain wants to see you."

Lee froze, wondering how she could have forgotten something as momentous as a possible murder charge.

One look at Shane's startled face told her that she wasn't alone.

"Seems Dillon didn't die from a broken neck," Grayfeather informed them. "The autopsy revealed that he'd suffered a massive heart attack before the fall. Too much fried chicken and cheap whisky." The officer's gaze shifted. He straightened, looking beyond Shane. "Here's Lynch."

Lee felt the bottom drop out of her stomach as she turned to confront Brandon Lynch. He was of medium height, with sandy blond hair and brown eyes.

He was dressed in jeans, a flannel shirt, and wore an expensive looking cowboy hat over his neatly trimmed hair.

And he wasn't alone.

A woman was with him, her dark hair and eyes triggering a shock wave inside Lee.

The woman looked familiar.

The man did not.

At least...not yet.

"Molly! Oh, thank God! Leandra, you're all right! And Molly...Daddy's little angel. Come here, you!"

"Glee!" Molly shrieked, reaching out for the stranger as he held out his arms. The woman was sobbing, clutching Lynch's sleeve as if she feared she'd collapse.

When Molly was safely in the man's arms, the woman grabbed the baby's face and kissed her until Molly squealed a protest.

While the woman and baby were occupied, Lynch tore his gaze from Molly and focused on Lee, his eyes moist and filled with happy relief. "Aren't you going to give your brother a hug, Leandra? My God, if you knew what a scare you gave us—"

Brother.

Lee's legs folded. Shane reached out and caught her in his arms, muttering a curse as he barked out a command for a glass of water and a chair.

Now she knew why the woman seemed familiar. She was Molly's mother, her sister-in-law. Molly favored her.

The room whirled and dipped, settled, then whirled and dipped again. Lee suspected she was on the verge of fainting, but she fought against it until she felt her mind gain an anchor.

She remembered everything, and the surge of information threatened to send her under again.

Brandon. Rose. Molly.

And Alec DeHart.

Shane's face swam into view above her. Lee mustered a smile at his worried expression. "Brandon Lynch is my brother," she told him, in case he hadn't been paying attention. Her voice sounded tiny, as if she was speaking from another room.

His sudden, beautiful smile made her heart do a triple somersault. Kyle Grayfeather slipped a chair beneath her bottom and thrust a glass of water into her hand before stepping back.

Slowly, Shane's arms left her. He moved a bracing hand to her shoulder as a precaution.

"What's wrong with her?" Brandon demanded. He handed Molly to his wife, then pushed forward to get to Lee. "Were you in an accident, Leandra? Grayfeather mentioned something about you getting lost in a blizzard—"

"Yes." Lee giggled, knowing it was inappropriate but unable to stop herself. She felt downright giddy as she stared into her *brother's* beloved face. Beyond his shoulder, she saw Shane watching her with an intensity she could almost feel.

"Leandra?"

She blinked, refocusing on Brandon's anxious face. "I was going to surprise you by driving up a few days early. You and Rose sounded so lost without Molly. I stopped at a gas station to change Molly, and left my wallet on the changing room table. When I went back to get it, I got lost." She glanced at Shane, biting her lip as she continued. "It was snowing so hard...I couldn't stop the PT Cruiser in time. I—I hit a tree, and Shane rescued us. Until now, I couldn't remember anything."

"My, God!" Brandon yanked her out of the chair and caught her to him, squeezing the life out of her. When he set her down again, he was crying. "When I think of what could have happened to you—"

"And Molly," Lee finished as understanding dawned. "I did a stupid thing, leaving without telling anyone. I shouldn't have been so reckless with Molly."

She knew, then, as guilt swamped her, why her memory had remained just out of reach. She hadn't *wanted* to remember her reckless adventure. Her mind had been protecting her.

"Alec must be out of his mind with worry," Rose said, grabbing Brandon's arm. "You should try calling him again. We couldn't reach him—"

"There's no need." Lee looked from Rose to Brandon, then to Shane as she added, "Alec doesn't even know I'm gone. We've been separated for four months. Our divorce became final a couple of weeks ago." Now that she'd stated the bald truth, she wondered why she'd hidden the news from Brandon and Rose.

They were adults, and so was she. Still, she felt she owed them an explanation. She licked her dry lips. "We—we just couldn't get along. We're too different." Alec had driven her crazy with his obsessive need to have complete control over her life. He had even picked out her clothes, scorning her more casual style of dress. The moment she'd left him, she'd replaced most of her wardrobe with denim and cotton.

If only she had known about his obsessive behavior *before* she married him.

Suddenly, Brandon was shoved aside and Shane stood in his wake, his gaze fierce and glowing. Slowly, he held out his hands.

Lee's entire body began to tremble as joy filled her. She wasn't married. She was free to love Shane, just as he was free to love her.

Uncertainty assailed her. But...did he? He'd never said he loved her.

She put her hands in his, rising to meet him.

His grin was crooked, sexy and shaky. "You're not married," he stated roughly.

"I'm not married," she said, grinning back at him. "Not anymore. *Alec* was the one who kept the canned goods in alphabetical order, and became enraged if I didn't keep it that way. I couldn't seem to please him, no matter how hard I tried. He's—he's a criminal lawyer. *I'm* going to be a public defender."

"It doesn't matter," he stated gruffly, "If you're going to run for Congress. I love you, Lee."

His whispered confession was heard by all.

Molly, who had been quietly watching them, began to shriek and fight her mother's embrace, perhaps sensing competition. "Glee! Glee!" she shouted, reaching for Shane.

Shane jerked his head in her direction. "Can we have a couple of these?" he asked, using one arm to pull Lee firmly against him, and the other to snag Molly.

Lee felt a wondrous sense of homecoming as she snuggled against him. She put her ear to his chest, listening to the strong, steady beat of his heart. "We can have a dozen, if you want to. Buck would like that."

"*I* would like that, too," he said, placing a tender kiss on her brow.

A word about the author...

Sheridon lives in Beebe, Arkansas, surrounded by family and friends, three dogs, and a horse named Dusty. When she isn't writing, she enjoys reading, playing with her grandkids, horseback riding, quilting, and brainstorming her next story.

Thank you for purchasing
this Wild Rose Press publication.
For other wonderful stories of romance,
please visit our on-line bookstore at
www.thewildrosepress.com.

For questions or more information,
contact us at info@thewildrosepress.com.

The Wild Rose Press
www.TheWildRosePress.com